The Virgin's Infiltrator

Black Hills Wolves Book 56

By
Dominique Eastwick

Copyright © 2017 by Dominique Eastwick
ISBN: 978-1-68361-085-4
Cover art by Fiona Jayde

Published by
Decadent Publishing Company, LLC

Look for us online at:
www.decadentpublishing.com

~A Note from the Author~

After writing *Infiltrating Her Pack*, I heard from so many readers wanting to know about Z's feisty and sarcastic twin brothers D and 7. I had no plans at first to write the twins stories but the more people asked the more they demanded until I couldn't focus on anyone else. This is D's story and I hope you love them as much as I do.

Happy Reading,

Dom
www.DominiqueEastwickAuthor.com

Dedication

Dedicated to all the readers who told me how much they wanted to know about the twins. Well here is the first.

Special thanks to Heather and Rebecca for letting me play in their world, and to Tracy who gets me through the real life work day.

As always thank you to Nadine who always pushes me to stop procrastinating.

Chapter One

Greystone Rafting Company....

Ripley, round with child, stormed in their direction. D poked his brother, 7, not sure what they had done to gain their sister-in-law's pissed-off expression. Running through the day in his head, he could not successfully think of a single thing they had done to anger her, at least not in the last couple of hours. They had, in fact, crossed off most of the items on her lengthy to-do list.

As she approached, he heard the familiar ringtone they had set up for their big brother, Z—an annoying and really loud roar of a T-Rex. "So help me if you don't turn this damned thing off, I will shove it so far up your...."

"Oh, she is worked up," 7 said, taking a step back.

"You think?" D stood his ground but only because it was his turn to take the scolding from Ripley, whatever it may be. They had made a pact as toddlers to share the load in all things.

"Well, you better go talk her down. If Z finds out she's worked up...." They both shivered, thinking about what Z would do.

"I'm not going over there." No one could call him stupid. Standing his ground was one thing, walking into the storm something completely different.

"It's your phone." 7 shoved him a bit harder this time.

"How can you be so sure?"

His eyebrows shot to his hairline. Reaching into his pocket, 7 pulled out the pieces of his abused device. "She took mine out yesterday."

"D, I'm not playing with you." She hurled the mobile at him, hitting him in the head. "Answer the damned thing before I tell my mate to send you back to records. And change the annoying alert. I nearly pee myself every time it goes off."

Another step toward the *Preganator*. He hesitated because they both knew she could, even months into her pregnancy, easily lift him and throw him into the icy-cold river behind them. Clicking the answer button, D leaned in so both he and 7 could hear the lashing headed their way. "Hey, Z, looking for me?"

"Why the fuck aren't either of you two answering my fucking calls, and why is my mate putting off angry vibes so strong I can feel them across the ocean?" Though his voice remained calm, the seething anger carried clearly enough.

"You cannot possibly know that." *How can he know?* D mouthed to his twin.

Their big brother growled through the phone line, "I do now."

"Shit."

"Put me on speaker when Ripley is back in the office."

They looked up to see Ripley standing on the decking about to enter her office. *How the hell does he do this?* Tapping the speaker button, they waited— patiently.

"You two need to head to Los Lobos and talk to the alpha there. His name is Drew. He has an assignment for you."

"Why us?"

"Because I found something here that might concern him."

"Wait." 7 smirked. "Are you saying you need us to come help you?"

"I think he is saying just that," D replied.

Z growled over the line, "Focus, damn it."

"We are focused."

7 wrung his hands in glee. "Focused on your need for our abilities. I suppose age is starting to catch up."

"Does Ripley know she has tied herself to an old man?"

"D." The word, like everything Z said, alerted the listener he walked a thin line.

Oh shit, too far. "Yes?"

"D is the only letter you will be filing if you don't shut up and listen."

D swallowed hard. "Right. Files. Listening."

"Listen carefully, I will not repeat myself. I. Do. Not. Need. You. But Alpha Tao does. It just coincides with where I happen to be." He could picture Z glaring at the phone. "You need to ask Ripley for one of the gift boxes for Gee. Do not open it. When you are done meeting with Drew, find Gee at the local bar and give it to him."

"Got it. Meet with Drew. Give token of affection to Gee."

"I have no issue sending both your asses back to files." Silence met his statement. The threat of being returned to filing old pack information in the underground circulation center silenced them every time. "One more thing. When you get to the border of the Tao lands, wait for an escort, and, no matter what, do not engage Ryker the pack enforcer."

"What fun is that?"

"It's about as fun as filing the letter E. Besides, he, unlike me, has no reason not to rip your jugular out."

"Understood." They chorused.

The line went dead. "Would it kill the man to use some manners?"

D ignored the hypothetical question. "At least we have an assignment again."

"About time." 7 removed his worn work gloves "Do you think Z cleared this with the council?"

"Do I think he went through the proper channels to get our time-out lifted? Absolutely not. Do I think anyone'll argue with him? No one ever has before. But he had to have suggested us to the Tao alpha."

"There is no way this Drew knew about us. I doubt anyone knows he has a family let alone a slew of brothers and sisters."

"Elusive, thy name is Z." He took a deep breath, glancing at the office modular. Very little scared him, but his sister-in-law petrified them both in her pregnant, hormonal state. "Do you think it's safe?"

"Have you silenced your phone?" 7 laughed.

"Yes, do you have chocolate?"

"It's in the office."

"How the hell are we going to get in there if the only secret weapon we have is beside the she-wolf?" D's phone beeped, alerting them to a text message.

Z- Check the outdoor first aid kit.

The two glanced at each other and strolled over to the metal box hanging on a pole near the winterized boat storage. Though the boats had a couple inches of snow over them, the kit only had a dusting. It had been opened recently. Inside, they found three wrapped chocolate bars.

Staring down at his phone, he wondered if his brother didn't have them tapped. "How the fuck does he *do* that?"

Tao Lands

D studied the two large wolves guarding the door to the makeshift office, more of a shack really. Using their internal connection, he reached out to his twin. *What do you think Z did to put these wolves so on edge at our presence?*

You've met our older brother, haven't you? He lives the whole bogeyman shit.

A tall, commanding man walked in—he could be none other than Alpha Tao. With a wave of his hand, he dismissed the two guards. When they hesitated, he lifted an eyebrow. As the door closed behind them, he addressed the new infiltrators. "So you're the brothers I had no idea existed."

"So you are the alpha our brother has so much respect for?" D asked, assessing the other man.

"Honor," 7 spoke, walking around the alpha.

"Integrity," D added, circling in the other direction. "But there is something else."

"A sense of responsibility."

"And not just because he is alpha."

"You are making me dizzy." Drew indicated the chairs in front of his desk with a jerk of his chin. Without waiting for the twins, he took his seat. "Your brother suggested, when I talked with him this week, you would be perfect for this job." He tossed a file on the desk.

They sat in unison, 7 reaching for the file. They read over the single page inside, titled *Natalie*. "This isn't much to go on."

"As it happens, Z thinks he has located her."

"So why does he need us?"

"I quote, 'I don't need them, but even I can't handle two warring packs and a sideshow.' I think he stumbled on the caravan by accident, caught a whiff of her scent, and went in for further inspection. Only conjecture on my part, as I can't get any more information from him other than he smelled Tao on her."

"Good to know we aren't the only ones he is evasive with."

Drew smirked. "You, too?"

"Ah hell, yeah." 7 glanced over the page again as if it would tell him something he'd missed the first time. "So he smelled Tao and thought to call you?"

Drew flexed his fist, frustration evident in his every muscle. This mild alpha would be a force to be reckoned with. "We have a lot of missing members. My pack is scattered. So, whenever he senses one of ours, he lets me know. I send someone from the pack to investigate."

"So why is this one different? Why us?" 7 asked the question they both thought.

"We've had issues in the pack recently. You might have noticed some fire damage. Resources are needed here. Sending someone to another country is not feasible at the moment."

It would have been hard to miss the pile of ashes and burned timbers in the center of town. *Issues seem to be an understatement,* D thought.

Agreed.

"Years ago, things got bad for our pack. Pack members scattered. Some couldn't get out. Others sent family members away. Natalie's parents died trying to escape with her when she was an infant. Someone, I don't know who, dropped the baby in her grandfather's lap to raise. Jonas, with his ability to come and go as a gatherer for the pack, managed to sneak his three-year-old granddaughter out one day twenty-two years ago. By then, the madness had all but consumed my father."

D absorbed this information. "Did Jonas escape?" *Did Z mention madness to you, 7?*

No, but when does Z share any information with us, useful or not?

Drew leaned back in his chair. "No. When they captured him, he told the hunters his granddaughter had wandered off and begged the alpha to let him continue his search for her. Smart move, as it guaranteed no one would spend a second on the child. We know now he'd left her in the care of a woman who lived a secluded life deep in the hills." Drew rubbed his neck muscles. "When Magnum died, Jonas went to find his kin."

"To no avail," D stated the obvious.

"No, but apparently she is wherever Z is."

7 leaned back, locking his fingers behind his

head. "Which is a mystery, as no one ever knows where he is."

"Well, he knows where he is," D mumbled. "But that doesn't really count now, does it?"

7 shrugged. "What did the old woman say?"

Drew looked from one twin to the other. "She claimed she'd sold the girl for a couple bottles of moonshine."

The twins froze, and D could feel the anger burning within his twin as brightly as his own. "Did she say who bought her?"

"A sideshow or circus. We had very few leads until Z called." Drew rubbed a hand down his face in frustration.

"Did they know she could shift?"

"My guess is yes." Drew stood by the window. "Jonas is dying, and his last wish is to see his granddaughter safe. It's a request I didn't think I could fulfill."

"So do we have a general idea where Z located her?"

"Europe."

7 groaned. "Could you be a little less 'Z' in this and narrow it down by, I don't know, a smidge?"

"Like a country or two?" D inserted before his brother could get his hackles any higher.

"There is a private jet waiting for you in Billings, Montana. Do you have passports?"

"At least"—7 held up his hand and started to count on his fingers—"five of them."

Drew leaned forward. "Five of them? Never mind. I don't want to know."

"Wait, did you say private jet?" 7 honed in on the luxury part while D worked out the distance between here and Billings, Montana. "You have a private jet?"

"Of course not."

"Z?" they chorused.

"That, you would have to ask him yourself." Drew led them to the door. "Not that I think you will get any more information than I have."

The twins took their leave and headed past a building at the center of town in the process of being built. The old town showed signs of revitalizations and rebuilding. The aromas of new paint and fresh-cut lumber mingled with the stench of smoke. They needed to drop the box off to Gee and be on their way to the jet. "Sev, I think we need to head straight out."

"Agreed."

Walking inside, they made a beeline for the bar. "We are here to see Gee."

"You've found him." The man turned, drying a glass.

7 sniffed. "You're a bear."

"You are a genius." The bear raised an eyebrow.

"Z neglected that information," Sev said with a snort.

"As Z is wont to do." When would he cease being surprised by his brother's evasiveness?

Gee tapped the bar. "You know Z?"

"All our lives," D said with a shrug.

"He is our big brother," 7 inserted.

"He wouldn't ever admit it, though."

"I can't understand why."

"We, after all, are quite loveable." D gave his most loveable grin.

7 batted his eyes. "Cuddly, even."

Gee resembled someone watching a tennis match. "You two are related to Z?"

"Why is everyone so shocked when they find out?" D eased his backpack off his shoulder and took out the box. "Here is your honey."

"Shhh," Gee hissed. "Z told you what it is?"

"Told us what? He said grab a box and give it to you."

7 wrinkled his nose. "Never understood the desire to eat bee scat, but, then, I'm not a bear."

You know it's not scat, right? D asked.

Of course, and though I personally think it's nasty gross, I wanted to get his hackles up. D knew his brother would be wagging his eyebrows in amusement if the bear wasn't staring them both down.

Well played.

"Did you open the box?" He turned it over, eyeing the seals.

"Of course not. As you can see, Z's safeguards are still intact. Why? Is this some big national secret?"

"What do you think?" The bear placed the box under the bar. "So, if Z didn't tell you, and you didn't peek, how do you know what's in it?"

His twin looked at the man as if he were addled. "We wouldn't be very good infiltrators if we couldn't figure out the contents of a simple box."

"Even with Z's protections?"

"Which we have spent our lives trying to break."

"Much of the time, unsuccessfully," D put in helpfully.

"I think I know why your brother hasn't mentioned either of you," Gee mumbled. "Will you be needing a room?"

"No, just dropping off this for Z. We're heading out of town."

"Good. I am not sure there is a vacancy. Give Z and Ripley my best when you see them." The bear indicated the front door.

"Enjoy your sticky spit." D smiled and followed his brother out the front door.

7 turned to glance back into the bar. "You know it's not spit either, right?"

"Just following your lead, brother." D patted 7's shoulder. "I don't think he liked us much."

"I can see why Z considers him a friend."

Chapter Two

Somewhere in Lithuania....

Natalie tempered her hatred for every human into her desire to rip the jugular out of the man holding the whip. She wasn't a dog to be trained and shown. Yet, six nights a week sometimes two shows each day, she and the other shifters acted like trained animals. Making the people believe the jackass Lee had any talent other than conning fools out of their money and enslaving shifters at a young age.

She would perform then pray they would leave her in peace for the night. Solitude was the only thing she hoped for anymore. The other shifters preferred to be together. But, then, most of the shifters who made up the circus now had been taken as infants and become a family. Lee had purchased her when she was old enough to have memories of a kind old man she called Gamps, a mean old wolf, and fleeing in the night. When she curled in her bedding alone, she could hear the gravelly old voice telling her she was special, she could be something. He loved her.

The animal tamer's whip sliced close to her flank. She turned and barked, baring her teeth. If only she dared rip out his throat. But they would kill her, and the others would be hurt, too. They kept her in line with two threats—the fear of the shock collar around her neck and harm to the other slaves. The collar beeped, its insidious sound warning her not to approach the human tamer. If she showed any sign of attacking, the collar would send enough electricity to buckle her knees. It only took one time to know she hadn't wanted to feel that pain a second time.

As she stumbled backward, Leonora the lioness eyed her with pity. Her fellow slaves knew she bore the brunt of the abuse.

Lee's wife, Shelley, approached and, in a low voice through the chain link fence, whispered, "Keep it up, bitch, and you will wish you were never born."

Her nightly wish already. What more could they do?

Settling back into her prison, she caught sight of the strange man with no scent who had snuck her food every day for the last two weeks. Three days ago, the bag had included a tube of antiseptic cream.

"For the cuts on your neck and hands." He left before she could shift and thank him. The food the first couple of days had been bland but still better than the slop she endured at the hands of her captors. But, soon, the food became richer, tastier, and, she suspected, as her full strength returned, full of vitamins and proteins she lacked. She didn't know if he visited the others, but she suspected he wouldn't only take care of her and leave them to rot. In either case, it wouldn't be long before someone would suspect something.

The Testas's viciousness knew no bounds. They would kill her Good Samaritan if they caught him. What was his story, anyway? He had to know she wasn't a simple wolf...the medicinal cream he'd included made that obvious.

The show wrapped up, and the audience left the old ratty tent. The group of human servants, so broken down they would do anything the Testas asked of them, remained. When the stranger approached the Testas, Shelley turned to those still in the big cat circus cage. "Don't any of you shift, do you hear me?"

Like they had a choice, with these damned collars on. She looked across the ring at the black bear, his hair hanging off him in chunks. Mr. Testa herded the elephants out the back exit to their enclosure. Not as easy to control as the cats and the bears, they posed a danger to the Testas's money-grubbing plan.

"Mrs. Testa."

"Mr. Zames." Shelley put on her best face—this man must have money and loads of it. Or she had the hots for him. Images of the two in bed made her nearly hack up a hairball. "What did you think of the show?"

"I only came in toward the end. Where is your husband?" Mr. Zames did not engage in small talk or acknowledge the flirtations of the woman. Nice to see his taste in people matched the fine suit he wore.

"He is putting the larger animals into the safety of their enclosures." Shelley sidled up to the man and rested her palm on his shoulder. "But I can help you until he returns."

"If I'm going to put funds into this ramshackle

circus, I need to inspect the livestock." Mr. Zames removed her hand from his person and stepped into the caged ring, showing no fear of its inhabitants.

Livestock?

"Really, you shouldn't be in there." Shelley's voice rose an octave.

"I have years of experience dealing with these beasts." Mr. Zames came closer to Natalia in her wolf form. She growled. He might have been giving her food, but she would be damned if he would fool her again. The damned man was in with the Testas up to his handsome neck.

Her collar beeped. Damn Shelley and her remote control.

"Relax. I'm here to help, Natalie."

In shock, she cocked her head. Although he didn't have her name correct, he was damned close. She lowered her head, allowing him to check her ears and whisper to her so the human bitch couldn't hear.

"Now, listen. I don't have much time." He lifted her paws to check the pads. "Two more like myself are coming. You must trust them."

She whined, trying to convey her concern.

He lifted her chin and opened her mouth as if to examine her teeth. "You won't be able to miss them. They bear no scent, much like me, but they are similar in appearance to one another. I have hidden food in the corner of your cage."

He patted her head and moved to the next animal, repeating the instructions until he had examined every animal in the cage. Some of these shifters had never felt a gentle touch before. They squirmed uneasily, but she kept them focused on her. She relayed her trust of him through a series of woofs and pants. She hoped they understood.

"So, what do you think?" Lee asked, coming to the center of the ring.

"I think your animals are malnourished and in need of some veterinary care," Mr. Zames answered, not bothering to glance away from the animal he examined.

Lee reddened. "If I could afford to pay to feed and care for them, I wouldn't need an investor."

"Yes, but when you have a bear whose hair is literally coming off in chunks, you make it difficult to believe my investment would go to the care of these animals." Zames indicated Shelley with a nod. "Those gems on your wife's fingers and ears aren't fakes and could go a long way toward getting care for your assets."

"How dare you? These are heirlooms."

"And those are living breathing beings." His voice never rose in inflection or tone, yet anger came off him in waves.

Lee took a step back.

"I have some other business I need to deal with. I will send out a vet this evening. The bear is in desperate need of medical attention. Do not prevent my man from working on the animals."

"And if the bear receives care…?"

"You shall get everything you deserve." His gaze locked with hers, anger flared for a moment. "I promise."

***

7 nudged his brother. "Here it comes."

Z walked out of the tent, picked up a trash can,

and hurled it over a truck twenty yards away.

"And he's pissed," D said.

"Always makes it so much more fun to deal with him." They'd been met by a chauffeured car at the airport and driven through the snowy landscape overnight and all the next day to a wooded area in the middle of Nowhere, Lithuania. Through the trees, they saw the tattered, faded tents and banners of the sideshow.

The driver passed them a note. After they got out and he drove away, D pulled it open. 7 hung over his shoulder, reading as well.

> I'm at the sideshow just on the other side of the trees you're looking at. Wait for me out of sight, and I will join you when it's time.
> Z

They killed time, at the side of the road, in the snow, wondering what awaited them in the circus tents. D noticed something odd in one of the tree trunks and peeked inside to see a box. He'd just started toward it when Z appeared through the trees. "Good, you made it."

"Nice throw," D informed him.

"If I had my way, it would have been the dismembered head of the asshole inside and his wife." He looked tired.

"Wow, that bad?"

7 eyed him warily. "What do you need of us?"

"I wasn't able to check the larger shifters in the back of the circus, owner Lee Testa took them off before I could get in. Of all the enslaved shifters, those are the ones I think are in the worst shape."

"Wait. Go back and repeat the last part. Enslaved shifters? You mean this circus is full of shifters?"

Z's nostrils flared. "Every last one of them."

D never had a great love of circuses to begin with, but enslaved shifters had his blood boiling. "We're listening."

"I have to be at a dinner function tonight for the Shestokus pack. If I'm not there, they will get suspicious." Z rubbed a weary hand over his face. "I need you to stay here and watch. I demanded the couple take some measures before I 'buy in.' The bear is in the worst shape of the smaller animals, but the female wolf, Natalie, takes most of the abuse."

"She is the one you think is Tao?"

He nodded. "She is definitely Tao, but I'm not sure she knows."

"Why don't we go in and kill the Testas and rescue the shifters?"

"Nothing in my life is ever easy," Z said. "The shifters are all wearing shock collars and, until we find out the source, as well as the perimeter markers, it's not safe to remove them. I don't believe some could withstand the shocks."

7 raised an eyebrow. "The great Z doesn't know something?"

"And he admitted it," D marveled.

"Even I can't keep two packs from war while trying to extract one of Magnum's goons from one of them to stand justice with the Tao pack."

"So glad you mentioned it. Who is Magnum?"

"And how did he go crazy?"

Z's eyes blazed then he calmed and nodded. "Magnum was Drew's father and the Tao alpha. He went crazy."

"That's it?" 7 demanded.

"Be happy with what little he is giving us, bro." D elbowed 7. No point in pushing their luck where their brother was involved.

"May I continue?"

The twins shrugged and nodded.

Z cracked his knuckles, a sure sign of frustration. "For the last week, I have been running between those two regal packs and this slum pit so I could drop food to those in chains. I'm not even sure the elephants have received the packets I threw over the fences."

"So we need to check on the pachyderms, find the shock-collar rigs, and check for possible booby traps, right?"

"There is one more thing. They are expecting Mr. Zames's vet this evening to check out the other animals."

"You don't expect one of us to play at being a vet?" D blinked twice in surprise.

"You can't be worse than a veterinarian those two asshats would bring in. I would come back tomorrow and find the elephants' legs sawed off and the bear without ears."

7 put out his fist, about to battle rock, paper, scissors style.

"I don't have time for this. My concern is they will pick up stakes and run by morning if they get any whiff there is no money. Or, worse, kill off the weak and move on with the strong. I think it wouldn't be the first time. They know shifters exist and pray on the weak ones." Z's phone beeped. He checked the message then let out a quick breath. "I have to go but will be back tomorrow morning. I've called in some help to assist us with the weaker, sick captives."

"Who?"

"None of your business."

I wondered when the real Z would come and play, D said telepathically.

Took longer than I expected.

I didn't expect any of the information we got.

He has been rather giving, for him, of information.

"You two keep chatting amongst yourselves. I'll see you in the morning." A second later, Z shifted into his black wolf form and raced off.

"Okay, you take the elephants. I will figure out the shock collars," 7 said.

"No way. I'm not sneaking into that cage. Forget the giant shit piles, those multi-ton animals spook easily."

Unless they spoke the same language, the elephants would likely trample whichever of them approached. "Rock, paper, scissors."

"You're on."

Double Rock

Double Scissors

Double Rock

Double Paper.

Why the hell do we even play this game? 7 asked.

No idea.

7 reached into his pocket and pulled out a nickel. "Call it."

Heads.

Damn it. 7 eyed the coin, shifted, and headed straight for the large animal enclosure. *This sucks.*

Well, it's gonna stink even more.

Auhhgg, you have no idea.

D got to do what he did best—circle the wagons and find the hidden security issues. 7 excelled at dealing with people., D sniffed the air catching and unfamiliar scent near the large cage. The circus must have been in town for a while. The hundreds of footprints would hide his in the snow. As he approached the decrepit travel trailer, a tingle started in his fingers and moved up his arm. *What the fuck?*

What? What did you find? 7 demanded.

Sorry. Nothing yet. What about you?

A lot of security and a lot of shit.

He worked his way along the tree line. If the enslaved being could get twenty feet from the camp, they would be home-free. The Testas had only bothered securing the directed radius around the circus. *Are the security guards shifters?*

Don't smell like they are. They aren't really good at their job.

What do you mean? D dismantled a crude trap on the outskirts of the camp.

Because I am standing right behind one, and he hasn't noticed. And, no, I haven't hidden my scent.

Are you thinking what I am?

Yeah. If they can enslave a shifter, what have they done to the humans? I'll bet every one of these security guards has been kidnapped or blackmailed into working for these two fuckers.

Takes Stockholm syndrome to a new level. Damn it.

Looking for a way into the enclosure. There was a brief pause. *Ugh! I wish I could send you smells as well as thoughts.*

Careful. The Testas are coming out of the tent.

With a line of emaciated people behind them. In the distance, elephants trumpeted.

Ooops.

Ooops?

Yeah. Though the elephants might be malnourished, they still have fight left in them.

D hid in the long shadows of dusk as the line of shifters in human form walked by like a chain gang. The old bear stumbled, hacking, and would have fallen had a lioness not caught him. "Get going, Balbus." A guard zapped the back of his leg with an electric prod.

"Stop it!" D stopped dead in his tracks on his way to attack the holder of the prod. The female voice sent heat soaring through his limbs and directly to his cock. But this wasn't a normal hard-on brought on by attraction. This was something more. He'd found the one thing every shifter both dreaded and anticipated. His mate.

Backing further into the shadows, he reached deep into his psyche to the years of training. Years of lessons to enable him to feel nothing, to show no emotion, and to stay neutral. He took calming breaths to suppress the growing need to claim the woman he hadn't even seen but only heard. *Fuck, fuck, fuck.*

What, what, what? 7 mimicked.

Closing off the ability for his twin to read all his thoughts, he focused on allowing him to only hear and see what he filtered to him. *We have a serious problem.*

On my way.

No, you continue what you are working on.

Seriously? Do you think I don't know you are

blocking me?

No. His brother would come no matter what now—if for no other reason than to annoy him. The icy snow crunched beneath the feet of the captives. Emerging from his hiding place enough to get a better look at the group, he stopped mid-step as a female, his female, stopped and glanced his way. After a moment, she caught up with the group and followed them until they turned to enter a large modular. Continuing forward, she removed a cover under the trailer wheel, revealing a small cage. Throwing her brunette hair with hints of red over her shoulder, she stretched once before yelping as an annoying beep sounded then climbed into the cage and locked herself in. Only then did she shift into a beautiful alabaster wolf and lie in the corner of the metal cage.

Why are you seeing red? 7 asked.

These shifters are treated worse than dogs. If he stuck to the truth, then perhaps he could hide the fact his mate was one of those being treated poorly. He wanted to keep this to himself, at least until he met her formally. He didn't need 7 meeting her first.

He could smell his brother long before he sensed him. *You reek!*

Do you know how hard it is to wipe elephant shit off your paws?

D sensed his brother shift to human form, but the smell remained as strong. *Try damn it!*

Who the hell is that? 7 asked over D's shoulder.

"I think it's Natalie." He didn't dare use their private path to communicate when they were so close and the connection was at its strongest. Better to do it this way—less chance of him giving himself away.

"She is definitely wolf."

"What gave away her secret? The fur or perhaps the tail?"

7 joined him. "Woo, who pissed in your coffee? I merely made a general observation. I think I'll go and check out the animals in the larger building. I should be able to pinpoint which is the bear, and the lioness. I'll call if I can't figure it out."

"Sev...wait. Fuck." No way this would work. He couldn't remember the last time he'd sniped at his twin. Ten years ago, maybe more. And now he wanted to tear his mirror image apart. If finding a mate made him this crazy in a few minutes, he would be happy to drop her off as soon as possible. But, in the meantime, he couldn't sit here and watch her shiver in a rusty steel cage. At a loss, he remembered the box in the tree trunk where the driver dropped them off. Perhaps it held something useful to their quest.

He waited until his brother entered the animals' trailer before shifting and heading at full speed to the drop-off place well up the road. Hidden inside the large tree trunk lay the camouflaged metal container. Opening the lid, he found a note.

Good, you found the supplies. Do not give too much food to the shifters at once. It will make them sick. Any items such as blankets need to be back in this box before the asshats wake up in the morning or they will question where they came from. Oh, and do not try a rescue without me. ~Z

After decades, Z still managed to surprise him with his abilities. *How the fuck does he do this?*

What did Z do this time? 7 asked.

He left supplies for all the shifters. Do you need

anything in there? D sifted through the supplies.

Don't think so. The elephants have not located their food, yet. I'll help them find it later. Z's right. They are in bad shape. But I can't communicate with them, so I can't get real close. They are feral at this point.

Can elephants be feral?

You know what I mean. It looks like big brother left food and meds for all the animals in the trailers. They're expecting us, but not for another day.

Good, then perhaps the Testas won't expect us either. Simply saying their name, even in his head, made his blood boil. Never had he come across a couple less worthy of breathing the same air as everyone else.

The bear's itching. Is there...?

Yep, some cream in a bag labeled bear. *Z is so frecking anal. He has stuff for each of the captives. Including new shoes for when they make an escape.* And a small metallic emergency blanket in Natalie's bag of goodies. Putting everything into a bag he could carry in wolf form, he closed the box and re-hid it before shifting and making his way back to the camp.

First stop, dropping off the cream. He entered to find all the inhabitants still in human form. 7 and a lioness held the paw of the black bear, preventing him from scratching. The poor creature had already clawed the skin raw. Shifting, he grabbed the bag before it could hit the floor. "Here."

The lioness looked up with grateful eyes. "I don't know who you both are, but thank you."

"Don't mention it."

"There is another one. Natalia. Can you check on her? They keep her close, under their mobile home."

The lioness smoothed on the ointment. "The guards circle once an hour, on the hour. They will check on her then, but, otherwise, they can't be bothered."

Thankful for any bit of intel, D checked his watch. He had twenty-three minutes before the guards' rounds. He left the building and made his way to where his destiny lay caged and shivering.

Chapter Three

Natalia sensed his approach long before she could hear or see him. This one she could feel deep within her, as if they held a connection. He had run all over the camp since she'd returned to her cage, and every time he had drawn near, butterflies formed in her stomach, only to dissipate as he passed her by. But, this time, he made his way toward her, and excitement buzzed within.

She shifted to her human form. The black wolf moved with a grace and agility she had never seen, carrying a bag in his mouth. Had she not been alerted to his presence by this odd internal alarm, she wouldn't have noticed him at all. He paused when their eyes met, as if he sensed this connection between them as well.

"Who are you?" she asked, crawling to the back of the cage.

He dropped the bag and pushed it until it hit the cage before moving back a few steps and shifting. Her breath hitched. She had dreamt of this man so many times she wondered if she was awake. "Natalie?"

"My name is Natalia."

"I think it used to be Natalie." His deep voice sent shivers up her spine.

"Who are you?" she asked again.

"My name is D."

"As in the letter?"

"As in the letter," he confirmed. His white teeth gleamed through the darkening night. He eased in so his back rested against one of the tires. She watched, entranced, as he brushed snow off his knees before focusing on her. "Do you remember your old pack?"

"Pack?" She remembered very little from before the Testas had taken her in.

"Your wolf pack?" His voice, though gentle and soft, held an edge of disbelief.

She rubbed the bridge of her nose. "I don't know what you are talking about."

He paused before continuing. "Take the blanket. You are shivering."

"I will, but David and Benji are due to walk through in a couple of minutes. They won't check on me more than once if I pretend to be asleep." She indicated a cluster of boxes behind her. "You can hide behind those until they pass."

"Do you not know what a pack is?"

She shook her head. She could read but only because Jill, another wolf, had hidden her own education from their captors. Jill took Natalia into her care, taught her to read, helped her fit in, and added some warmth in a life of frigid loneliness. Like all the shifters, Natalia had hawked cheap souvenirs, popcorn, and hot dogs until the shift happened at adolescence. Then they went from indentured servants to slaves. The collar went on. Jill explained

28

they could never let a human see their change; she helped her through the first few moons. She didn't want to remember those teen years. After her fourth moon, Jill had disappeared. Natalia, a mere teenager, found herself in charge of aging elephants, bears, and a slew of young shifters who had yet to reach adolescence.

"How much do you know about your kind?"

"Very little." She couldn't hide it. She hadn't seen another wolf shifter in ten years, since Jill left. Not until she saw D coming at her, and then she knew immediately he was like her.

"A pack is a wolf group. It's your family."

"I have neither."

"That's not true." D sniffed and shifted and, a second later, disappeared into the darkness under the trailer, taking the bag with him.

Her shift was far slower, and she lay down in the corner of her cage at the same time the cage door opened. The odors of the two guards filled her nostrils. She didn't need to see them to know they squatted and gawked, as always. "She's asleep."

"Shame she is a freak. In human form, she could be such a hottie, if they would feed them something. But I would never fuck an animal."

"I'd fuck her. Right up the ass."

Swallowing the bile forming at the back of her throat, she was overcome by a flash of red behind her eyes as well as warmth embracing her. The darkness returned as the two men walked away. Only then did she open her eyes to see the black wolf, hackles up.

She took advantage of his distraction to check him out. She itched to reach out and run her fingers through his thick, shiny black coat. The color rivaled his human form's hair. So black it appeared blue. He snorted then shifted. Their eyes met before she could turn away.

"Blanket." He crawled over to where he had dropped the bag and shoved the blanket through the slot in the cage. When their fingers met, a spark lit the dimness. "You are freezing."

Freezing? Her skin burned from the residual jolt. Unfolding the metallic sheet, she pulled it around her shoulders.

"Damn it," he groaned, unlocking the door and climbing in with her. He removed his coat, placed it over her, and pulled her into his arms. "You are shivering so loud the Testas are sure to hear you. How do you manage?"

Her teeth chattered. "I stay in wolf form. But even that isn't enough."

He wrapped his arms tighter around her, tugging the jacket and the sheet over them both. "Do they not give you a blanket? Heater? Anything?"

Coffee. He smelled of coffee beans. Her lids fluttered closed as an unfamiliar sense of security flooded her, combined with a warmth she had nearly forgotten possible. Exhausted, she murmured, "I am being punished."

"For?"

"Trying to escape." Curling into her dream protector's arms, she let sweet sleep take her.

***

The battle between lust and the all-consuming need to tear the two people in the building above them apart, piece by piece, warred within him. Her breathing evened out, alerting him she'd entered REM sleep. His feet had long ago lost feeling, and he had sweated more in the last hour than he had in years, but his mate slept soundly and, he believed, in warm comfort for the first time in he couldn't begin to guess how long.

He couldn't see her shock collar, and his fingers had yet to find a way of getting it off. At one point, when he placed a finger between it and her skin, the item beeped. Natalie tensed, as if anticipating the shock to come. He ran his fingers through her hair until she relaxed once again in his arms.

Well now that escalated quickly, 7 said, laughter in his voice.

So caught up in the new sensations rushing through him, he completely missed his twin's approach. *She will be hypothermic by morning. It's well below freezing.*

Need me to take over so you can stretch your legs?

His brother embracing his mate? Not hardly. *How are the others?*

There is no way they can escape on their own. Maybe the lioness, but even she isn't in great shape, and certainly not in this weather. 7 leaned against the same tire D had earlier. *I can tell you they spent a hell of a lot of money on these shock collars, and, until we find their controllers, they are stuck here.*

In the morning, one of us will need to get into the building above us.

You think the shocking bay is up there?

It's the only place I can think of. If I were them, I would keep it close to where I slept.

Okay, then. Since you seem to have a sleeping

partner for the night, I'll take another look around. See what I can find.

Have fun with that.

Tomorrow night, I get to hold the pretty lady while she sleeps, and you can maneuver the minefield of elephant dung.

D's inner beast roared. No one would hold this woman, not even his brother. The fierceness of his reaction shocked him. And from his twin's wide eyes, it shocked 7, too. "Holy shit," he whispered.

"Hush."

7 approached the cage. *You found your mate?*

It appears so.

Does she know?

I don't think so. She senses something, but I don't think anyone in this camp has a mate, and as we were briefed on the way, they were all brought into this life of servitude so young, none of them have the knowledge to understand what happens when a mate comes along.

Do any of us know what to do when it happens before it happens to us? Do you?

He shrugged. The elephants trumpeted, followed by a second more frantic sound. 7 shifted and ran full out toward the elephant enclosure. *Damn these assholes.*

Do you need me?

I'll let you know when I get there.

D adjusted his mate so, should the need arise, he could get out there to help his twin as soon as possible. The door above them slammed open and then slammed shut; the whole trailer shook with the power of it. *You have company coming your way.*

Of course I do. A minute later, 7 cursed. *Lee is*

here with a prod. Fuck them. I think they are trying to rile up these shifters so if they end up dead in the morning, they can try to convince Z the animals are at fault and not them.

D snorted. *I would love to see anyone try to pull one over on our big brother. I am on my way.*

No, wait. I don't want them to know there are two of us. To be safe, stay there. Your mate needs you.

His mate? Wow, seemed odd to have his brother speak of it so easily when he was still coming to terms with it. *Okay, but the first sign you're in trouble, I'm coming.*

Fair enough. *I am assuming where elephants are usually from in Africa they are speaking Shona. How I wish I had paid attention in our foreign language classes just a little. There might have been a chance at least I could communicate with these two.*

D didn't speak a word of Shona. He didn't doubt Z did, but his expertise didn't help them. This woman who grew up here had to know some words to communicate with the other animals. She spoke to lions, so maybe she could also understand the elephant. He shook her gently. "How would you tell the lions to calm down?"

Natalia's eyelids fluttered open. "*Podza*, why?"

"Curious. What about friend?"

"Are you planning on hitting on the lion?"

"Not at all…. I am trying to say the word friend."

"What about Andile?"

"Andile? Is that how you say friend?"

"No, Andile's the female elephant's name. Are you planning on hitting her? I promise she is pretty attached to Urayai."

Trying to get information out of a half-awake sleep-deprived woman while being vague was confusing them both. Perhaps the straightforward approach would be best. "Can you tell me what friend is in Shona?"

"What the heck is Shona?"

"It's the language local to the areas where those elephants likely came from, and probably the lion. So can you tell me how to say friend so I can help them without being trampled in the process?"

"Oh, try *shamwari*. It should work." She snuggled into his chest and fell back to sleep.

7 sent him a thought. Fuck! I am not a vet, and I don't have the knowledge to pull this off. But I did find the bag Z left outside the enclosure. I guess none of these assholes have ever seen a vet working on their prisoners, so how would they know if I know what I am talking about anyway.

Sev, try—

I actually doubt any of these have a fourth grade education, let alone a doctorate in veterinary studies. Is that even a real thing? I need to research it when I get back.

Sev, you need—

Perhaps I can use the vet gig as a new way to get into packs. How crazy would that be? Dr. 7, animal doctor.

Shut the fuck up! Okay, mental yelling was a bad idea. His words bounced around his head over and over.

What? And ouch. Let's not do that again.

D rubbed the bridge of his nose, wondering if

they annoyed everyone the way his brother annoyed him right now. He could imagine Z saying yes and cringed. *When you approach the elephants, use the words* podza *and* shamwari.

When did you start speaking Shona?

I don't, Natalie does. Well, at least a bit.

You didn't happen to get their names, did you? Not the ones these idiots call them. Somehow I think calling them Kimbo and Jumbo isn't going to go over well.

Urayai and Andile.

All righty, going silent. If you sense I have passed out, I suggest you come because it means my chest is under the very large gray foot I am staring at right now.

The likelihood the large animal, even in the best of health, would outmaneuver his agile brother seemed unlikely. He hadn't seen them shift and wondered if 7 had.

Have you seen them in human form?

Busy.

This is important. Are they even strong enough to shift?

Dude, I'm really trying to focus, so unless you have some big vet words to help...shut your brain down.

He had never left his brother out on his own like this. One always had the other's back, and had this woman in his arms not been gifted to him by fate, he would be out there now, too. And 7 knew it. *I am coming out.*

No. I need you to stay where you are. One of them said something about taking care of Natalia in the morning. I got this. You take care of her so I don't have to split my attention.

He didn't say anything.

D, I am serious. Your feelings are all over the place, and you aren't on your game. But you don't have to be on your game to protect her. Your instincts will kick in for that.

Infectious canine tracheobronchitis.

What?

It's the only term I know.

Kennel cough? They are neither in a kennel, coughing, nor canine.

So leave out the canine, and they won't know the other words, but it will make you sound smart.

His brother went silent for a few minutes.

How did you know what the term meant?

Remember the time I hid from Z in the med ward? Woo, it smells in here. I can't believe these two are forced to live like this. I could strangle those humans with my bare hands.

Calm down. Tell me about your time in the med ward. Anything to take 7's mind off the anger he could feel through their connection.

Right, um we played some stupid prank on Z.

They were never stupid, D conceded to himself. Perhaps some of the pranks might have been dumber than others.

They were all stupid. Anyway, he caught me mid-prank the way he always does and I ran and hid. He locked me in a cage and said he would send someone to get me.

Did you catch kennel cough? D searched his memories but couldn't remember the event. He had a vague recollection of his brother and him being apart for a while. No punishment had a bigger effect on them than separation.

I did, damn him. Okay I need to try and get some food into these two. And I don't trust they aren't poisoning them, so I need to find the other bags of food hidden in here, and I am afraid they might have relieved themselves on the bundles.

Have fun with that. D snuggled Natalie closer to his chest, quite content to have his assignment under the trailer and not in a minefield of dung.

Why do I get all the glamorous jobs?

Better than filing?

Debatable.

Natalia awoke alone and without a blanket to find D closing the gate. "Sorry, they have just awoken above us. I didn't think it would bode well for me to be there with you. At least not until we can get that blasted collar off you."

Well rested and colder than she had ever been after a night of warmth, she felt the chill more acutely. She also had a sense of loneliness accompanying his retreat. "Why do I desire to touch you when all other men make me want to hit them?"

"We don't have enough time right now to go into a conversation you will have a ton of questions about, but I promise if we haven't figured out how to get you to safety by this evening, as we sit here in this cage again, I will tell you anything you want to know."

"And if we get out of here? What then?"

"I will sit in a safe, warm room and tell you anything you want to know." He indicated the small brown bag beside her. "Eat quickly before they come. Don't eat or drink anything they give you. I will return for you later."

"Where will you be?"

"Within hearing distance." He reached through the cage and cupped her cheek. "I will never be far, even if you can't see me."

"I can sense you, why?"

"Because, we are mates." He put a finger to her lips. "No time."

He shifted and gave her one last long glance before he left seconds before the cover was pulled off and sun flooded in. She wanted to asked what the hell he'd meant by mate? Needed to know why they seemed connected. She would have called after him, but the overwhelming sweet yet acid scent of Lee Testa's cologne assaulted her nostrils.

Lee kicked the cage, not even bothering to check if she still slept. "Get up, Natalia. We have a very important day, and I need you in human form to help convince Mr. Zames to sign the deal. I think he is waning in his desire to add funds to the circus."

"How can you trust me not to mess it up?" Fumbling, she shoved the brown bag of food into the waistband of her pants.

"Because, if you do, the others will suffer. You are too soft, Natalia. Now, get up. You need to bathe and put on clean clothing. You also need to convince the others to be on their best behavior. One wrong step, and I will kill them all. Then you. I want you to see them suffer and die. Now get the hell out here."

It took her three tries to open the cage with her shaking fingers. Testa gripped her forearm so tight, she lost feeling to her hand and cried out, unable to prevent herself.

"Shut up, you stupid bitch! If you are good, you

might get an extra portion of food."

As he dragged her behind him, she caught sight of the black wolf on the edge of the tree line and took strength from his presence. She didn't know what being a mate meant, but she figured in some way they were meant to be together. His keeping watch over her gave her fortitude. She entered the staff quarters, which were better than her living conditions but not by much. On the bed farthest from the door lay a rumpled dress and underwear with the price tag attached.

"Take a shower. You smell like the stables." He handed her a few bottles and a bar of soap. "Take these toiletries, and the clothes are yours. You have twenty minutes before I come in and dress you myself."

"I understand, sir."

"Good." He turned back in the doorway, eyeing her. "Come here. We don't want to make a bad impression." He took a key out of his pocket and removed the collar. "I don't think you need this. You understand I will kill everyone if you try and ruin things, and if you run, I will track you down and kill you with my bare hands." Touching her neck, he tsked. "There is a scarf under your new dress. For God's sake, cover the red marks on your neck." He left, taking the evil device with him.

Natalia turned on the water in the shower and gobbled the food D had given her. She couldn't remember the last time she took a warm shower, even lukewarm. Anything would be better than the tub they gave her for a hip bath every other day. She jumped in and let the water flow over her. The sweet smell of the rose shampoo assailed her senses and she massaged it into her hair.

"You have fifteen minutes," one of the guards yelled through the thin trailer walls. "Or you can take it slow, and I can help you dress."

She slammed the nozzle into the off position. The threadbare towel did little to dry or cover her body. Better for her to be clothed and working on her appearance when they came in than naked. It had been years since she last had new clothes. And although the dress could be categorized as gently worn, it was new to her.

When the door opened, she still struggled to get the zipper up her back. Mrs. Testa stood there and tsked. "Let me help you."

"Please, ma'am."

"We need to do something about your makeup and hair, too. Your appearance wouldn't seduce a blind man, let alone someone as sophisticated as Mr. Zames."

Mr. Zames didn't want to seduce her, but she couldn't and wouldn't tell Mrs. Testa he had spoken to her on more than one occasion. "Seduce?"

"My husband is convinced you are the ticket to getting the money. So it's time to earn your keep. On your back, if need be. Sit."

Natalia followed the direction. Better to pretend to be malleable, or at least willing to do as she was told for the sake of the others. The brush yanked through the knots. Shelley Testa didn't care if the hair ripped from her scalp.

"He's here." Mr. Testa stepped into the trailer.

In frustration, Shelley ran the brush faster through her hair. "I haven't gotten her makeup on yet."

He smirked. "Perhaps for the best. Maybe her innocence will be such a commodity, Mr. Zames will overlook her other obvious flaws. Tie the scarf around her neck. Not too tight. If she is fidgeting with it, he might get suspicious." He grabbed her chin in a tight squeeze. "Do not blow this. The bear dies today if you fail."

"Yes, sir." She averted her eyes to prevent his seeing the disgust she held for him. He had seen her antipathy before, but she had strength this time. Food and rest had recharged her.

They emerged in time to see Mr. Zames getting out of his car. She saw no sign of D, but she could feel him.

"Good morning, Mr. Zames." Lee's sugary greeting would attract flies.

"The animals?" Mr. Zames demanded.

"Your vet has been in the large animal enclosure all evening, taking care of the elephants."

"And the bear?"

Wow, this man would not give Lee an inch. She rubbed her nose to cover a smirk.

"I'm not sure."

The stranger eyed the two Testas, eyes blazing. "You don't know, or you won't say? I suggest you take me to the bear, now."

"But—"

"Now."

For the first time, she saw the man she loathed and feared retreat like a coward. He bowed and rushed to the trailer where the other shifters lived. Shelley would have sent a three-beep code, informing them to shift and get into their cages. The Testas asked for a second to go in first and, to her surprise, the other man nodded.

When they were alone, he whispered, never looking at her, "Are you all right?"

"Yes, thank you."

He leaned in and sniffed her. "You're covered in D's scent. Interesting."

Taken aback, she tried to act nonchalant. "How well do you know D?"

"I've known him all his life."

"Oh." She wished she could ask a hundred questions, but there was no time. Nor did it appear this man would answer much of anything. "He says we are mates?"

"He's correct."

"How would you know?"

"Because, as I said, his scent is all over you, and no matter how many showers you take, another wolf would smell it." Mr. Zames turned and took the stairs into the trailer, not waiting another minute for permission to enter. Natalia followed out of concern for her friends and, to be honest, she felt safer with the wolf. Not as safe as she had with D last night, but close enough.

She eyed the other shifters as she followed him in. They fidgeted more than normal. Balbus lay on his side outside of his cage. She moved to run to the old Kodiak's side, but Mr. Zames stopped her. "Send someone for my vet."

He didn't wait for anyone to answer. People followed this man's orders without question. He pulled out his cell phone and spoke in what sounded like the local dialect, but she couldn't be sure. He seemed to be giving the person on the other line a list of some sort.

D entered, and she took a step forward then shook her head, confused. This man was not her mate. As he passed her, he murmured, "Not D."

She gasped, sucker punched. Twins! "Not D" moved over to the bear and crouched. He turned away, his nosed crinkled in disgust. "We need to get fresh bedding in here."

"On its way." Mr. Zames approached, reaching into his jacket. "Here are the antibiotics you requested."

"The pachyderms are stable."

"Good to know." More went on in this conversation than the three to four words each spoke. Balbus, though still in bad shape, showed signs of improvement from the evening before, and the open sores on his paws seemed to be healing. Both men continued to work on the patient, apparently oblivious to anyone else around them. She could sense D moving around the camp. Unlike the other two newcomers, who moved as if invisible, she could feel D as he got near.

They used Balbus as a diversion.

"He found it," the other D said in a conversational manner, but she picked up a slight hint that the three words held a world of meaning.

"Good. I'm going to check on the truck." Mr. Zames headed for the door. "Lee, walk with me and we can discuss finances."

The Testas visibly relaxed at his words.

"Can your...I'm sorry I have no idea who this woman is to you."

Lee pulled Natalia forward. "This is our foster daughter, Natalia. Perhaps after dinner she can give you a private tour."

"Natalia, it's a pleasure." He moved in to kiss her cheeks, first the left. "Are the others stronger shifted?" he whispered. Then the right. "We move out tonight." He backed up. "Perhaps, at sundown, you can show me around?"

"It would be my honor to show you whatever you wish to see." She looked to Shelley for approval and noticed the other woman had left. "Shall I stay in here until you need me?"

"I could use the help," D's twin answered from the corner, indicating the bale of fresh hay in the corner.

Making sure no one remained who might cause them issues, she asked, "What do you need from me?"

"I need you to stay put and safe," he answered, patting Balbus on the back. He crossed the small space and grabbed the broom. "You can get up, old friend. But stay in your animal form to continue healing. All of you stay shifted and get some rest. You are going to need it tonight."

"What about their collars?"

The man pushed the old hay out from under the bear before stepping back to allow Natalia to spread some new bedding. "I think your mate has that well in hand. I'm 7, by the way, in case you're curious."

"Seven?"

"It's a pack thing you wouldn't understand." 7 kicked some more hay out of the way and sat on the floor with a yawn. "Damn. I'm tired. Mind keeping watch since you managed a good night's sleep?"

"Watch for the Testas?"

"No," he yawed again, "they don't scare me. But my big bad brother Z does."

"You know they're going to try and kill you all?"

He shrugged, pulling his knees to his chest and resting his arms followed by his head on top. "They can try, might make this whole thing more interesting. Not much so far beyond long piles of shit."

She would have questioned his idea of interesting, but he fell asleep quicker than she could get her thoughts together. Instead, she looked out the only window in the trailer. Showtime at six thirty would come soon enough. And, usually, they would be in the tent cleaning and doing manual labor by now. The others used the unusual free time to sleep and heal. Something none of them ever had enough of—keeping them malnourished and exhausted helped keep them all in line. It also meant none of them ever worked to their full potential.

The security guards sat out on the old pickup truck bed, smoking cigarettes, not focused on anything other than their conversation. It must have seemed like a break for them, too, as they had all the animals contained into two locations and not around camp working. Z and Lee walked around now and again. They spent close to two hours in the tent before heading to Andile's enclosure. She wasn't close to those two; an inability to speak their language had put distance between them all. Leonora had taught her the few words she knew, but the lioness said she had been traded from one freak show to another since she was a child and admitted to remembering very little of her former language.

"Why are you still here?" the lioness asked, in human form, sitting outside her cage.

Natalia stepped away from the tiny window. "I

thought you were sleeping."

"Nah, I got some sleep last night. Amazing how a full belly and warm blanket can help." The other woman sat on her cage, out of sight line of the window. "Do you know what is going on?"

Natalia shook her head. "I think they are planning something for tonight."

"Why are you still here?" Leonora repeated. "You're in clean clothes, your collar is off...you could be long gone by now, and no one would be the wiser until later."

"They'll kill you."

"They can't kill us. We're as they say a 'cash cow.'"

The door opened, and Natalia turned, her stomach churning in guilt, as someone entered. The youngest of the security crew stepped inside, with a tray of food. 7 jumped up in front of the two women before she knew he had even woken. "I brought food. For you two. Leonora, it's a good thing it's me, and not one of the others. Be careful, okay?" The young boy's tender heart would get him killed one day.

"Billy, what did you bring?" Natalia took the tray from him and placed it on top of Leonora's cage.

"I brought food for the doc here and Mr. Zames requested some food for you, too, Natalia. You can imagine how Shelley viewed that request. I also brought a few extra items I could sneak in for the rest of you."

Leonora bit her lip. "You shouldn't have. If they find out...."

"Well, they didn't, so stop worrying." He reached into his pocket and pulled out a stained napkin. "I found some blackberries out in the woods. I know

Balbus loves berries. Maybe, when he wakes up, you can give them to him?"

"You are really too kindhearted for this place." She took the napkin and laid it next to the sleeping bear.

"I'd better get back out there before it raises suspicions."

"Are there any other guards worth saving?" 7 asked when the door closed.

The taut tone and the way he stared at the door as if he could see through it told her he needed a straightforward answer. "No."

"Good. Makes things easier."

"Easier how?"

"It's probably best if you don't know. We've so far not seen much to redeem the humans in this group."

Other than Billy, Natalia had no redeeming experience at all. But she didn't feel comfortable thinking the wolves were going to kill them. Z didn't strike her as someone who hesitated to take a life if the need warranted it. D and 7 she couldn't read as of yet.

The door opened again, and closed before she saw who entered. But she didn't have to put eyes on him to know D stood in the shadows.

"This is a dangerous idea of yours, brother."

"I have been in worse predicaments." He grinned, coming out of the darkness of the entrance.

7 walked back to his sleeping spot. "I have been there with you and remember them with great fondness."

D cupped her face with his palm. "Are you hanging in there? Your neck is raw."

She closed her eyes, the touch charging her.

He ran a finger under the scarf and growled when he saw the chafed skin.

7 threw the ointment at them as if D had asked for it. "This doesn't smell great but it will help."

He poured a liberal amount into his palm and started to apply it to the sensitive skin. "Z said he could smell you on me."

"I would have been shocked if he hadn't."

"Good lord, you can smell it a mile away," 7 mumbled into his arms never raising his head.

She lifted her arm to smell her skin. "Is it permanent?"

"No, it will fade." He moved through the trailer, checking the shifters, a long pause before his next question. "Are there anymore somewhere else? Anyone else they might be punishing as they are you?"

"No, just us and the elephants."

"Okay." Another long pause.

7 huffed.

"Can you two communicate telepathically?" Leonora asked.

"Why would you ask that?"

Natalia had wondered the same thing.

The lioness looked between the two male wolves. "There was a set of twins in one of the traveling groups I lived with. The bird sisters. They would use them to cheat at cards or do parlor tricks. One would ask what card someone held or what they drew, and the other would sit on a perch behind the unsuspecting victim."

"Oh." Natalia hadn't known bird shifters existed nor had she realized telepathy could really happen.

But she noticed neither of the twins said anything to confirm or deny. "Well?"

"Well, it's time for me to sneak out again. I just saw the patrol pass. I'll see you in an hour or two. Sunset should happen at four ten, 7, and the moon will be half-full. So there will be some light, but not a lot. I suggest you get some rest. It's going to be a long night." D reached up and touched her cheek before heading for the door.

"Will you be coming back?"

"Not in here, but I'll see you later. I promise. 7. You okay in here?"

7 raised a thumb in answer, and D slipped out, leaving behind an uncomfortable silence.

Chapter Four

Sundown....

Natalia hadn't moved from her post at the window since D left. She could still sense him moving around the area. He would stop for minutes on end then suddenly be at another side of camp as if he'd poofed there. She hadn't once caught a glimpse of him, though, and neither, she suspected, had anyone else. Z finally came out of the tent and spent some time on his phone. Lee talked at length with his security guards, certainly about how to kill Z and 7 when the money finally arrived. She hadn't seen Shelley since morning and, for a woman who liked to be the center of attention, her absence screamed odd.

The door opened, and Lee came in. "Showtime."

Natalia didn't need to be told what he meant or who he referred to. He expected her to help seal the deal. She took in her fellow captives, knowing it might be the last time she saw these. They might not be much, but they were the closest thing to family she had. She wished she could hug them and tell them she loved them all, but she couldn't alert Lee, and she wouldn't. This was the group's best chance of escape.

"Hurry up, girl. The supply trucks have arrived. I need him busy when they come."

She could only imagine why, and every thought brought worse images than the ones before. "I don't have my coat."

"You won't need it. I'm sure he will keep you warm enough." Lee smirked and gave her a creepy wink.

Z waited at the opening to the tent. She couldn't read what he thought, and she wasn't sure if the chill running down her spine had to do with the cold or being with him.

"Natalia."

"Mr. Zames."

Lee pushed her the last few steps. "She works the show tonight, so, if possible, please have her back by curtain time."

Z nodded and removed his long wool coat, placing it around her. She followed him deep into the woods. She'd never been allowed past the clearing. She looked back at the camp, the only home life she had ever known. Not the place, but the camp itself.

"Never look back," Z whispered. He stopped and pulled her into his embrace. Every fiber of her being fought his touch, his closeness. "Relax, we are being watched."

"I can't."

"Neither can I."

"What do you mean?" She searched his eyes, hoping to find the answer she doubted he would give her.

"This feeling of disgust isn't yours alone. Just as

I'm not your mate, you are not mine." With an arm wrapped around her, he moved deeper into the dark woods. Snow crunching beneath their feet provided the only sound on the windless night. "Besides, that display was twofold."

"How do you mean?" she asked when he finally released her so she could take a step back.

"Not only did it make all watching believe the scam, it acted as good as a distress call for your mate. He should—"

"I'm here." D stood, his chest rising and falling in a display of male prowess.

"Easy, boy, she's all yours." Z patted his brother on the shoulder. "Get her out of here. Follow the scent markers I have left for you every click. They will lead you to a safe house. In the basement, there's a false floor leading to an apartment farther below. I left the standard charm on the door along with the security system. You will be innocuous there, and Sev will join you as soon as he can."

"I can't leave him in there alone." The distress in her mate's voice for his twin was clear to them both.

"You can't leave her alone. She is your main concern. 7 and I'll get everyone else out. My suppliers are a rescue team. Kaleb and his crew will take the others somewhere safe and secure to allow them to heal."

The sound and smell of a human approaching stopped them.

"You deal with this one. I need to get back. Until we meet again," Z said and, in a blink of an eye, he shifted into wolf form and part of the night.

D hid her behind a large larch tree. He placed a finger to her lips to silence her and locked eyes with her as the footsteps grew closer. As the guard walked past, D grabbed the man by the neck and slammed him into the tree.

As D reached back with a fist ready to strike, Natalia stopped him. "No! Billy is the only one who has ever been kind to us. Ask 7."

He relaxed his grip but remained between Billy and her. "Human, you need to run in the opposite direction from the camp and don't stop until you reach town."

The boy stared. With the hand still wrapped around his neck, he couldn't vocalize his thoughts.

"He has no money, nowhere to go. Can't he—"

"Absolutely not."

"Why did you come out here?" she asked, removing D's hand from around the boy's throat.

"I had to make sure you were safe. When your kind is taken into the woods, they never come back. I worried. I knew I had to help." The poor boy trembled, yet he'd put himself in danger to save her.

"Oh, Billy. You could have gotten yourself killed for me."

"I had to do something. I couldn't let them hurt you." Big brown eyes showed the young hero who lay beneath.

D reached into his back pocket and pulled out his wallet. He handed him a big wad of cash and a card. "You get into the next town. It's about three clicks that way. Stay off the road. If someone stops you, show them this card. If you make it to the town, you find a place to lie low. Order room service, but do not come out. The number on the back is a lawyer. In the morning, you get in touch with him. Tell him you are calling in regard to a Japanese lantern. He will understand."

"But I don't understand." Billy looked at the card as if it might explode.

"You don't have to. Now, go, before it's too late."

Billy eyes became the size of saucers as he shoved the money into his front pocket. He went to say something else but thought better and ran as hard as he could.

"Come on. We have to go." A warm hand wrapped around hers.

"What about Billy? Won't they track him?" She dug her feet in, concerned.

"No, I've already told 7 what is going on. He will let the others know." When she refused to budge, he groaned. "Sev had already let everyone know to be on the lookout for Billy. He'll be fine. I promise. Tomorrow, when the air settles, I'll check on the boy."

The sound of screams rent the air. "What was that?"

"You don't want to know. Come on. We need to get out of here. Do you run better as a human or wolf?"

"I have never run as a wolf."

"There is always a first time. Shift now." D shifted.

She followed as best she could. He ran through the brush, stopping every so often to let her catch up. She didn't hesitate; she let her wolf side run free and untethered. The wind rushed through her fur and her heart pumped. For the first time, she truly felt alive.

Unused to the activity, as they neared the other side of the field, she fell head over tail into the embankment. A yelp escaped, and D rounded back and shifted back to human form. "You did great. We're almost there."

She shifted, too, her whole body shivering in reaction to the exercise. He lifted her easily into his arms and continued running through the night. She clung to him, unable to argue and unwilling to resist.

Ten minutes later, they came to a small shack in the woods, as dilapidated as if it hadn't been inhabited in this century. He pulled the squeaking door open and ducked as a bird flew past. Lowering her to her feet, he took her hand and led her through the house and down to the basement. A well-hidden door in the floor became visible after D chanted in a language she didn't understand. It opened with a click, and lights below turned on. He gestured to a ladder leading downward. "Can you make it down there?"

She nodded, but just as quickly shook her head, swallowing the lump in her throat. She had escaped one cage to be placed in another. "I don't want to."

"This is only temporary. But we need to get you in there where it's safe, warm, and there is food."

The ladder grew before her eyes. She could do this, one rung at a time. Closing her eyes and holding her breath, she descended the small tube leading to what might be hell. Once her feet hit the floor, she opened her eyes and moved out of the way. D soon followed chanting again. A door appeared in the wall with a blue light next to it. The door slid open at his touch. "See, it's not so bad."

"Better than what I had before." She prowled through a suite of rooms and ended up in a compact kitchen. "Is it okay to have some water?"

"Help yourself. Fix a meal, just take it slow. And

I want you to take a long, hot shower or your muscles are going to cramp up."

"Where are you going?"

"I have to cover our tracks. Since I carried you the last bit of the way, I just need to divert them from the clearing. Hand me your dress if you would?"

"What?"

"Your dress; it has your scent."

"I am not getting naked in front of you." Yet the thought was far from repulsive. A strange warmth spread from her belly down to the apex of her thighs. Images of them undressed, limbs entangled, flooded her as well as a sudden urge to strip down and tear his clothes off.

He went into one of the three rooms connected to the main one and she heard water flowing. A moment later he emerged. "There are several sets of clothes in there for you, new undergarments as well. Go in, take off your clothes, all of them, and then go into the bathroom. Once you are in there, I'll take the clothes you've left on the bed and use them to take your scent elsewhere."

"Okay." The small room she entered had enough room to walk to the bathroom, but the bed reached from wall to wall on three sides. A flat-screen television was mounted next to the bed on the far wall. Inside, she found five sets of women's clothing, all in different sizes. Each consisted of two pairs of jeans, T-shirts in blue, purple, and black, a brown sweater, and a dark-gray winter coat. On the floor lay five pairs of assorted hiking boots and a similar number of shopping bags containing underwear, bras, and pajamas. She reached out and picked up the softest pair of pajama bottoms she had ever felt.

"You all right in there?"

"Yes, um...?"

"What?"

"What size do I wear?"

He remained quiet for a minute but tapped on the door as if thinking. "If I were to hazard a guess, I would say about size six."

She grabbed the bag marked six, and when she flipped the card open, although her reading level was that of a young child, but after a minute she could make out it read:

Natalie,

I hope something in here fits. If you need to, mix and match until you find what works for you. If nothing is perfect, we can get you something else when we get you home.

~Z

The extent of what had happened started to rush over her. The clothes the Testas gave her suddenly burned and she wanted them off her body as soon as possible. She stripped the clothing off, ripping the dress when she couldn't get the zipper down, and kicked them nearer to the door and farther from her.

The small and utilitarian bathroom left no room for frivolity; everything had a purpose, not like the one Shelley had in her trailer. She much preferred this one. Before closing the bathroom door, she yelled out he could come in, and, as the steam filled the room, she stepped into the shower and sighed.

"You don't mind if I burn these when I am done, do you?"

"I would actually prefer if you did." She let the

water wash over her, only barely conscious of the sound of the bedroom door closing behind him.

D gripped the dress and discarded undergarments in clenched fists. The wolf in him demanded he go into the bathroom and claim his mate, but he knew she didn't understand. He would scare her off, and he didn't want to take a chance. He grabbed for the zipper bag to hide her scent until he needed it then placed the plate of food he'd prepared for her while she went through her clothes on the table. Next to it he laid two ibuprofen for the pain and a glass of water.

Pushing through the barriers of the house, he tried again to reach his brother, but he hadn't heard or felt his presence since they reached the clearing. This was the farthest the two of them had been from one another ever. He hoped, once he got out of the safety of the building, he would hear from 7. The four screens showed nothing but a raccoon padding through the house and nothing outside. He was loathe to leave her, but this had to be done.

Leaving the room, he reclosed and secured the door before making his way through the house. He shifted, and the clothes never hit the floor before he had them in his bite. Running full speed, he hid his scent. The night air smelled of snow, and he wanted to be back in the shack before it hit. When he reached the clearing, he shifted again, took out the dress, and coated the area with their scent going in the other direction. He had purposefully guided her over and through the frozen stream to divert anyone who followed. He took the stream until it opened into the lake. Running around the edge, he found what he looked for, a thirty-foot waterfall. Wrapping the dress around a large rock, he dropped it over the edge.

7?

Nothing, not a murmur or a vibration in his brain. A very large part of him wanted to go find his brother, but the other part needed to be with Natalie, to protect her. Never before had he felt so divided. But he had to trust his brothers could take care of things on their end while he cared for his mate.

He made sure all tracks were covered and there weren't any scents he might have missed on the way out. By the time he reached the front door, the first flakes danced to the ground. As he entered the safe room, Natalie sat on the sofa wearing light-green pajamas with lots of moose all over them. The plate he had left lay empty, he noted with satisfaction, and she jumped to her feet when the door closed. "You're back."

"Did you think I had left?"

She fidgeted from one foot to the other, biting her thumbnail. "No, I just didn't realize how long you would be gone, and I couldn't sense you."

"I think it has something to do with the walls. I'm sure Z has figured out something to prevent even connections like ours from getting through."

"What is our connection?"

"We are mates. I know you don't quite understand."

"Tell me, then."

He led her back to the sofa. "Fate, the goddess.... I guess no one really knows who predetermines our mates for us. If we are lucky, we find them. Sometimes our mates come to us when we most need them; sometimes when we are least prepared."

"So we—the two of us—were determined to be mates even at a young age?"

"At birth."

"I belong to you now?"

"No, we belong to each other, if you decide it is what you want." He sat next to her on the sofa; he needed to touch her. Grabbing her hand, he brought it to his lips. "We can take this as slow as you need."

"What if I'm confused about what I want?"

The need to mate was clearer than anything had ever been in his life. He could not understand how she could not feel the same. The sense of certainty flowed through him like the blood in his veins. But she wasn't in touch with her wolf side, and patience was his only option. "Explain."

"I want to run. I want to be out in the field and run."

"Hopefully, tomorrow, it will be safe enough."

"And I want space, lots of space, but at the same time space scares me. I've never had it, so it terrifies me...like you." She turned back to him. "I want you to touch me in places no man has ever touched, and yet I don't know tenderness, and your being nice scares me. I don't know how to trust this bond."

His cock came fully alert. "Have you never been with a man?"

"No. I kissed a couple of guards over the years, and an occasional person who came to the circus, but I've never had sex with anyone. I've never wanted to, but...."

"But what?"

She leaned forward and locked her lips on his. He allowed her a moment of control before his wolf took over then he pulled her into his lap, taking the kiss deeper. This moment he and she were created for. He wondered now why his pack settled for being with those not their mates. Never going out to find those destined for them. Because nothing compared to this embrace.

He wanted to be naked. He needed to feel her breasts against his chest without the annoying barrier of clothing. The images of her naked beneath him, legs locked around him tight as he pumped into—

"Woo! Didn't need that in my head," 7 said, closing the door behind him.

Natalie jumped off his lap as if 7 were her father and they teenagers caught in the basement. Annoyed at his twin's interruption, he was equally relieved. Both to see and sense him. Covered in blood and all.

"Are you all right?" Natalie asked before he could.

7 nodded, running his hand over his face. "I don't think any of it's mine. But I can't be sure."

"You killed them, didn't you?"

"We killed those who would have killed us."

Fingernails bit into D's knee as she came to terms with those words.

"The Testas?"

7 took a deep breath. "Shelley Testa is AWOL. But as much as I'd liked to have dealt with him, Z had his mind set on the mister."

"So he is dead?"

"Oh, every last piece of him is dead. Z is nothing if not thorough." *It wasn't pretty. Be glad you had her far away. I've never seen our big brother lose his cool. But he tore that human man to pieces. He took his time doing it, too.*

"Can we expect Z back anytime soon?" D asked.

So the man felt it all?

Oh, he felt it. "No, he had to get back to some social event. The man has powers that still astound me. After all was done, Z shifted and looked like he came out of the spa, not an epic battle."

"Why don't you take a shower, and we will get some food ready for you." D needed to keep the conversation on the lighter side and find something to keep Natalie's mind occupied. Many wolves didn't deal well with violence, but most understood some beings had no redeeming value. The Testas were among those he was quite happy to have wiped off the planet.

"Sounds like a plan." 7 started toward the first bedroom, sniffed the air, and moved on to the next one.

Only when the door closed did D turn to his mate. Knowing the only father figure she had, even as the father from hell, had just died in a violent manner might not sit easily on his gentle she-wolf. "You understand Lee was a danger to shifters? And, more importantly, to you."

She nodded.

"The way he treated you isn't okay in any world, and this is one of the few times we as infiltrators are allowed to take life without question."

"I'm not questioning the need to deal with him and most of his guards. They had no redeeming qualities."

"But?"

"But if Shelley is still out there—" Her lips quivered in fear.

"She will not get you. Do you understand?" He placed a finger under her chin and tipped her face up toward him. "And the others are safely out of her grasp."

"What about Billy?" She gripped his arm to make sure she had his attention. "He's young and never accepted how they treated us. He tried so hard to help, but he is just a boy. They treated him worse than us."

"Do you want me to see if he has called the number yet?"

She nodded. He could do nothing more than make sure his mate's concerns eased. He pulled out his cell phone to text his sister. Damn, no bars. He kissed her lips and moved into the corridor, immediately getting a signal.

D~ *Did a man named Billy contact you?*

N~ *Affirmative.*

D~ *Is he safe?*

N~ *For the time being. Z will extract him tomorrow and take him to another of his safe houses until a plan can be made. We're tracking any family down now. Billy, like most in that circus, seem to have been abducted as children.*

D~ *Thank you.*

N~ *Wait. Did you just thank me? Did you hit your head or something?*

D~ *Or something.*

He shut his phone off and returned to the room, securing the door behind him. "He's safe, and my sister is searching public records for any family he might have now."

"Thank you."

D moved into the kitchen and threw a sandwich together for his brother. "You don't have to thank me. Did you get enough to eat? Do you want another sandwich?"

"I ate more this evening than I usually eat in one day. This place, what is it?"

"It's a safe house." Leave it to his brother to have it fully stocked. "I can promise you my safe houses are nothing like this." Perhaps he should talk to 7 about working on those.

"You have a safe house?" She leaned a hip against the counter, watching him work.

"7 and I have three."

"How many does Z have?"

"Lord knows. Hundreds, maybe more." He searched the refrigerator for a beer. Finally finding one, he placed it on the counter. 7 deserved it.

"Really?"

"Really. He's been out here for about a month, getting this one set up as needed, I guess."

"Why do you need safe houses? I mean, I might not know a lot, but I know this isn't the way most people live—appears as if no one lives here at all. You don't even have a scent when you don't want it."

"We are infiltrators." He pulled out a bag of chips from the cupboard and opened a container of cookies, offering her one.

She shook her head. "Is that a pack name?"

"In a way, but it's more an ability. We are watchers, and protectors, but don't make the mistake of thinking we are on anyone's side."

"Are you the good guys or the bad guys?"

"We are normally neutral. We can't interfere in other packs and we cannot assassinate alphas, no matter how evil or crazy they are."

"Alphas?"

About to ask if she was kidding, he paused when

the seriousness of her face alerted him she really had no idea, and he didn't want her ever to feel she couldn't ask him a question. "Alphas are the leaders of the pack. Strongest male, though I think some women could be amazing alphas."

"So, would Lee be an alpha?"

"No. Lee was an asshole. Sounds close but not the same." 7 came out of the room in nothing but a towel, shaking the remaining dampness from his hair.

Where the fuck are your clothes?

"Thanks for the sandwich." 7 reached around her for the plate and the beer.

How about you go back to your room.

His brother took a giant bite of his sandwich.

If you choke at this moment, I will not save you.

Ah, it's not like there is anything in me she wants. I'm not her mate.

We are mirror images.

Are you afraid she'll want me?

No.

You are. Classic.

"Are you two talking?" she asked.

"More like thinking." 7 sat down, continuing to demolish his food. "It's very handy."

"It's a bit annoying right now," D said pointedly.

To D's relief, she moved toward him. "Must be strange never to be alone."

"It's our normal. Tonight's the first time in our lives we couldn't hear one another." 7 echoed his feelings. "And you did a hell of a job with the false scent. Threw me for a second."

"Did it?"

"Yeah, then I realized you had spelled out Z. You

suck raw eggs, dude. I knew I was on the wrong trail."

"You caught that, did you? I thought it added a nice touch." D laughed.

7 stood, stretched, made a show of a yawn, and excused himself. *Let the seduction begin. Just please try and block images and keep it down.*

Natalie's shoulders slumped and her eyelids drooped as exhaustion set in. Any seduction his brother thought might happen tonight would have to wait. "Why don't you head to bed?"

"It's been an exhausting day." She moved to the bedroom doorway. "I can't remember ever sleeping in a bed."

He saw red. He only wished he had been the one to kill Lee. The treatment she and the others received at his hands just kept getting worse. And although he cared about the others, the treatment of his mate made him angry beyond words.

"It angers you, doesn't it?"

"It does."

"I'm sorry."

"For what? You were—are innocent."

She bit her lip. "Will you sleep with me?"

"What?" The words barely made it past his lips.

"You held me last night, and I felt safe and warm. I know in my head we're safe, but I'm worried when I fall asleep, he'll be there waiting for me in dreams." How could a woman strong enough to stand up and fight such evil be so fearful? But then, she had seen some things no one should have.

"I will hold you every night of our lives if that's the only way to give you peace."

What the fuck! You just gave me diabetes. Really, bro? What kind of game is that shit. Take her to bed and let things move the way fate meant them. Now, shut me out for the evening, please!

You could always go sleep in the woods tonight.

Do you know how cold it is out there?

Exactly, so stop complaining.

When he followed her into the bedroom and reached to close the door, she stopped him. "I feel a little like the walls are closing in."

He smiled and turned on the flat screen. The image of the outside came to glowing life, making it appear as if the room didn't lay below ground but overlooked the backyard through a big window. "Better?"

"Wow." She reached up to touch the screen.

He shut the door before taking the one step to reach the bed. While she marveled at the falling snow before her, he turned down the bedding, let her choose a side, and climbed in behind her fully dressed. "Are you really going to sleep in your clothes?"

"Unlike you, my brother did not supply me with a closet full of clothing." He usually slept in the nude information he didn't think would ease her mind., . "I'll be fine."

"I'm not sure I can sleep with all these layers." She shimmied out of her bottoms and gave him his first real look at her long, muscular legs.

"What are you doing?" Panic set in. He needed to be a gentleman, and she needed a knight not a horndog, but the more clothing she removed the closer he got to the latter.

"I've rarely had a blanket, let alone several layers of clothing, and the sheets are so soft I want to feel them sliding over my skin."

He gritted his teeth trying to control his hormones. But when she removed his shirt from his waistband, he knew his mate wasn't likely to be a virgin by morning. "What are you doing?"

"You need to feel these sheets, and you can't do it with these clothes on."

"You're playing with fire," he gritted out.

"I know."

Their eyes met, and he realized she might be naive about a great many things. But, here, now, she knew what she wanted, and seducing him seemed to be at the top of her list. He didn't fight her but didn't assist her as she removed his shirt and pulled it over his chest. Her fingers brushed over his skin leaving a trail of goose bumps in their wake. "Do you have any idea what you are doing?"

"No. But I'm doing what feels good, what I've seen others do and never thought I'd want to."

As much as he wanted this, he sensed she wasn't ready. "You want to do what?"

"I want to make love to you."

"Do you understand what that entails?"

"I'm a virgin, not stupid. I've lived under a damned trailer most of my life."

He put a finger to her lips. "Please don't mention your living conditions, not right now."

"It bothers you. I'm sorry. Anyway, I've been informed as to what to expect."

"Why don't we do this? You lead tonight. We'll take this as far as you want. You say stop, and we will." He leaned in and kissed her. Not because she wanted it, but because he needed it. In all the crazy of this trip and this night, he'd realized having a mate meant putting her above him, and putting her needs first.

It might kill him, but letting her explore his body might allow her to be more relaxed later. He had no doubt they would be intimate, but he didn't think she was emotionally ready to lose her virginity. Too much had happened tonight for her brain to be working at full capacity. He didn't want her regretting a decision. She and her wolf weren't in tune, not yet anyway.

She would need time and space to get to know who she could become, and although it went against every fiber of his being, he had to give her all those things. She nipped at his neck, and he shivered.

She drew back, an adorable furrow between her brows. "Why do I want to bite you?"

"Bite or nip?"

"I guess nip."

"It's your she-wolf. When wolves mate, it's more powerful and rough than most humans."

"So I'm not a freak?"

He gripped her shoulders. "You are not now and never have been a freak. You're from a magnificent race, and it's unfortunate life has dealt you a shitty hand. But you will come to understand there is nothing wrong with you. And, anything we do together, as long as it's mutual and agreeable, is fine."

Her gaze flicked away. "Do you really believe what you're saying, or are those words to make me feel better?"

"I never lie, ever. Most wolves can sniff out a lie miles away." He ran a finger down the delicate line of her collarbone. "Even when we are in the field, we keep things truthful. We go by names rather than letters and numbers, but the more truth you keep, the easier it is to infiltrate a group. You become trustworthy."

"So you deceive with honesty."

"Funny how that works." She fidgeted with her shirt as if undecided if she could remove it in front of him. But he could smell her desire and sexual need coming off her in waves. Sexual frustration mixed with the adrenaline and uncertainty became a crazy mixture. He could take care of at least one of the items. "Do you trust me?"

Without hesitation, she nodded.

"Good. I want you to place your hands on the wall...no, on your knees." He gripped her hips and maneuvered her into the position which best worked for what he planned to do. The white silk panties would need to remain on. If she wasn't ready to remove her top, the underwear would be worse. "I want you to focus on the falling snow on the TV screen."

"Okay, but—"

"No buts." He pushed the hair off the nape of her neck and kissed the sensitive skin. "All you have to do is enjoy the ride."

He lay on his back, inching his head between her spread thighs. "Trust me."

With her silk-covered most intimate lady parts within inches of his mouth, he closed his eyes and let her scent fill him. Lifting his head, he blew a breath against her and gripped her butt cheeks forcing her to stay still. When she moaned, he took a chance moving the silk with his teeth and baring her to him. Before she could argue, he licked her clit, holding her in place as she squirmed to move away.

Sucking and licking, he drank from her, and every moan and pant drove his need to please her further. Her orgasm hit her so strong, he felt her ecstasy as clearly as if he had come. He reached up and, within a second she lay below him, her legs spread wide and his cock replacing his mouth. He pulled back from her, panting for air. She lay like a goddess against the gray sheets. "We have to stop."

She came up on her elbows. "What?"

"If we continue, there's no way you'll leave this bed a virgin." He sat on the edge of the bed with his back to her. If he caught sight of those thighs again, his honorable intentions would fly out the door.

"I'm okay with continuing." A warm hand touched his tense back.

"You'll also not walk straight for a week. Your safety is more important than my need to brand you."

"Brand me? Is that what this is about, making me yours?" She moved away from him until her back hit the wall.

"No." He threw a blanket over her bare form, too tempted to see even an inch of her porcelain skin. "But, if we continue, I'll be unable to control my need to make you mine in every way I can. You are not ready for it. No matter how much your body is ready to be sexually awakened. I cannot do one without the other."

She stared down at his erect cock, outlined through his jeans. "You can't be comfortable. I've heard the guards complain about blue ball...."

"I'm going to take a shower, and then we'll both try and get some sleep." Goddess help him maintain his honor.

Twenty minutes later, he came back into the bedroom to find his mate fast asleep, clinging to a pillow the way she had clung to him the night before.

Had he been smart, he would have let her sleep and taken another pillow to the sofa in the main room. But he wasn't smart when it came to Natalie. He eased the pillow from her grasp then slid in next to her. Immediately, his cock came back to life. He cursed inwardly but knew there was nowhere else he would rather be. Closing his eyes, he let blissful sleep fall over him.

His internal clock told him it was close to two in the morning when he awoke to the sounds of pounding above them. He opened his eyes but otherwise remained still and listened to the sounds around him.

"What—" she began.

He snaked an arm around her neck covering her mouth with his palm then pointed above, bringing a finger to his mouth before releasing her. Her chest rose and fell rapidly as the seriousness of the situation came over her.

Do you hear what I hear? he asked 7, hoping his brother had awakened.

Yep. I'm watching the security cameras now.

Do you need me out there? Need me to lead them away from the house?

No to both. These are local police. Someone must have discovered the caravan. Although the bodies are long gone, there might be traces of blood we missed.

Not to mention the missing Testas. He was never more thankful for this silent connection. He didn't want to remind Natalie that Shelley Testa roamed free somewhere out there. He played with her hair. She had to know he communicated with 7, and he hoped it eased her mind.

I am sure they're just investigating wherever they can.

Let's hope so. Yell if you need me.

I will. Just keep it quiet. Although I think Z set this room up so you could hear footsteps but they can't hear us, I don't want to test it.

Agreed. He mouthed for her to sleep, and she nodded with her head on his bare chest. He couldn't see her eyes, but she wouldn't sleep anytime soon. *What are they doing?*

Right now, they are heading into the basement. But it would take a world-class detective to figure out the cracks in the floor conceal a hidden door.

How many?

I counted five. There might be more outside in the woods. But the snow is still falling, making it hard to tell what is what on these cameras. Okay, they are leaving the basement. I think the investigation is over. I'll stay up in case they track back.

Wake me if anything happens.

He kissed the top of her head and whispered, "They are gone, but we need to remain quiet for a bit in case they come back."

"Who was it?" Panic edged her voice.

"Local cops. Who knows why they are here, or if they are looking for anything in particular." D knew they were looking for someone or many someones, but he didn't want her worried any more than she was.

"But we are safe?"

"Yes."

She snuggled into his embrace and, within a few minutes, her breathing slowed into a calm rhythm. D stared at the ceiling and listened.

Unlike the evening before, where she barely moved within the security of her arms, she tossed and turned, murmuring in a restless sleep. The blankets lay at the foot of the bed. Every time he laid them over her, she kicked them off again. She definitely didn't like having her feet covered. He lay like that for hours, eyes open and nerves stretched taut.

"Good morning?"

He smiled down at her. "Are you asking if it's good or morning?"

"Morning. I can't tell if the sun is up or not." She indicated the TV he had turned off during the night.

Another example at how out of touch she and her wolf were. "It's morning. The sun rose about an hour ago."

"Why do I feel so secure with you? Like I belong." Though the words should have brought relief, an underlying sense of everything being too overwhelming prevailed. She had never been able to rely on anyone.

"You are the other part of my being."

"Forever?"

He stroked her hair. "I think so, but, to be honest, I'm not up-to-date on my soul mate information."

"So I go wherever you go?"

"For the time being, it would probably make sense, but we are taking you to your grandfather. You're part of the Tao pack. They are your family, and they are anxious to meet you."

"What if I don't want to go to the Tao pack?"

Honesty was best. "Your grandfather is sick. He doesn't have much time, and his last wish is to see you safe at home."

"So I belong to them?"

"I'm not sure what you mean by belong? Yes, you belong to them, in a way. You are family, but they don't own you."

"No, you own me."

"No, I don't." He wiped a hand over his face, praying for strength and enlightenment to say the right thing to her. "I'm your mate. It's different."

"How?"

He climbed out of bed. "Fate declared us a couple."

"So, once again, I have no choice in my life." Panic edged her voice.

"Do you feel trapped with me? By me?"

"Yes...no...I don't know. I just want to run and never stop."

She'd spent her life bound by a collar, in a small cage, and suddenly she has her freedom and was stuck again. She sat in the bed they had slept in, the sheets pulled over her breasts, looking lost and very confused. "I'm not going to demand you go anywhere with me. But you can't stay in this country. Once we get you home, I'll give you the freedom you deserve." The words nearly killed him to say.

"I want space, but at the thought of not being with you, I can't breathe."

"You've never had the chance to be alone. It's your time. I'll be there when and if you are ready. But I have to get you to a safe place first. Beyond making sure your grandfather talks to you, I doubt Drew will keep you hostage in the pack."

"I need space," she repeated again but at a higher pitch.

"Let me go and do a perimeter check. If it's clear, I can let you run. Your safety has to come first. You understand?"

She nodded. "You don't deserve this from me. I know in my head you aren't my enemy, but in my soul, I...."

"You've been through a lot, and nothing about this is fair." He grabbed his discarded clothing. "Get some more sleep. I'll take a shower, make some breakfast for you, and then check the area around the house."

"D...."

"Don't worry. It's okay." But it wasn't. His world shattered at the idea of her choosing not to be with him, and he couldn't do anything about it. If he kept her tight to his side, she would resent him. He had to let her run; he had to let her have the freedom she had never experienced. No matter how much it killed him to do so.

Chapter Five

"Where's D?" 7 asked when she came out of the room an hour later.

"I thought you could tell."

"No. There is something about the building preventing our connection from, well...connecting when one of us is outside the safe room. But I did sense frustration in him this morning before he went silent. So where did he go?"

"He went up to check if it's safe. I want to run."

He paused mid-pour in his coffee. "I see."

"What do you see?"

"I see that even though it would be safer to remain inside out of sight until Z contacts us with the time to get to the airstrip, he went out where it's dangerous to allow you to do something any idiot knows is a bad idea." He finished pouring his coffee and brushed past her. "What I see is, my brother no longer has any sense."

"He said if it's not safe, I can't go up."

"Trust me. He'll make it safe."

"And that upsets you?"

"Upsets? No. Pisses me off? Yes." He crossed the room to watch the security screens. "And if something happens to him, I have to stay with you, as you are my mission."

The door to the outside opened. "What's going on in here?"

"That is the question. Why the hell would you go out there without telling me?"

7 could have had a private conversation, but he wanted her to hear him.

She had been selfish and acted like a spoiled child. Guilt racked her. "7, I'm sorry."

"What does she have to be sorry about?" D demanded.

7 remained quiet, and somehow she knew this time they weren't communicating. "I shouldn't have asked you to go out. I wasn't thinking."

"No, you can ask whatever you want. 7 should have faith I can take care of myself as well as my mate."

"Faith in you? When have I ever questioned any move you made even when it landed us in the fucking basement filing hundreds of years of files? When, D?" He slammed his mug down. "But that move"—he pointed to the screens—"when you know the police could be watching, and there are people looking for her...it was damned stupid. What the hell are you trying to prove?"

The two men stared at each other.

Then 7 bit out, "No, you say this out loud. She should hear this."

"We're done with this conversation." D stormed out into the bedroom they'd shared and slammed the door behind him.

"This is the first fight my twin and I have ever had." He glared at her. "Somehow, I don't believe it will be the last."

"I'm sorry."

"So am I." He pointed to one of the screens. "There. Right fucking there."

A stocky police officer came out of the wooded area. "Do you think he saw D?"

"I know he didn't, but he would've seen you. And you would've ended up under arrest as a prime suspect in the disappearance of the people from the circus. I don't want to have to break you from prison." He gulped the coffee. "Especially a foreign jail."

"Why would they think I had anything to do with it?"

"The question you need to ask is why they wouldn't. I guarantee Mrs. Testa went straight to the police to say you threatened her. Her passport hasn't been used, so she is still in the country." He pointed to the camera on the lower screen. "He suspects this house isn't all it seems. Five dollars says he comes into the basement."

"Ten, he goes upstairs first," D said from the doorway.

"You're on."

D pressed a finger to his lips, and she nodded then watched on another screen as the officer moved through the house, weapon drawn.

"What was that?" she asked as a black blur moved across one camera then the other.

"Z," they chorused.

The police officer dropped to the floor, limp, and Z came into focus. He pointed to his watch then left the camera's view.

"If there is anything you want to take, I suggest you get it now," 7 said, shutting down the monitors.

D went into the bedroom and returned with one of the winter coats. He helped her into it. He'd selected one that fit well, she thought, apropos of nothing. "Come on. We have to go. If Z shifts, Natalie, you shift, too, understand?"

She nodded.

"Stay to my right. If we hit trouble, I will circle you. Do not shift back to human form unless we say so. If we get into trouble, stay behind us."

"Everyone's safety is relying on you following what he said to the tee," 7 added as he shut down the power systems.

She felt like she might vomit. "Okay."

"You wanted to run. Just think of this as a run and you'll be fine."

"We won't let anything happen to you," 7 said, opening the door and indicating the ladder. "Ladies first."

Z reached from above and helped her up. "Shift now."

She nodded and allowed her wolf to come forward. She hated the shift, it hurt, and, for so many years, nothing good had come from being an animal. D and 7 came up, and all three shifted together. A trio of black wolves led the way out of the house. Z paused, sniffed the air, and made a beeline across the field for the tree line. D and 7 took her around the house, staying out of sight. After all, one wolf had gone in, so it made sense one would come out.

They moved slowly around the perimeter, making little sound.

D blocked her from moving as 7 moved forward but froze a few feet ahead of them. She took a step, and D huffed. She froze, lowering her head. Human voices in the distance caught her attention, but they were too far to understand their words. A wolf howl rang from the east and the voices cut off. Pounding footsteps, crunching leaves underfoot indicated they raced in that direction. She, 7, and D loped in the opposite direction.

Her legs burned from ill-use, and tears filled her eyes, but she couldn't stop. Shifting was not an option, either. She pushed until her legs gave out and she rolled headfirst into the snow, crashing into a tree. She hadn't finished her shift, when she found herself in the human arms of D. He raced after his brother.

"I. Can. Run," she panted.

"No you can't," he answered without even being short of breath.

They came to a road where a black limo waited, the engine purring. A rear door opened, and Z stepped out. How had he gotten there so quickly?

"He can throw his voice." D put her down, but she stumbled, and he picked her up again and climbed into the car. She nearly jumped when she came face-to-face with a man tied and gagged sitting across from them.

7 entered, followed by Z. "Meet our traveling companion. He has some questions to answer back in Los Lobos."

The other man struggled against his binds. 7 leaned in to examine the knots. "I wouldn't do that if I were you. It's like a Chinese finger cuff, the more you fight, the tighter it gets."

"He's a wolf. Why would you have him tied up," Natalia asked, trying to catch her breath.

"Just like there are bad humans, there are bad wolves." D kept her tight against him. She happily remained in his arms, especially when her arms and legs started to shake.

7 handed her a bottle of water. "Drink this. You need to hydrate." He removed his coat and placed it over both D and her. 7 was a conundrum; he didn't like her, yet didn't hesitate to protect her and see to her well-being. It had more to do with his brother than any mission.

Z sat near the window, working through some files. He sent a few texts and took out a map. As they passed a sign indicating they neared the airport, Z reached into his pocket and handed her a passport. "It's yours, and it's legal."

"How?"

"Best not to ask," D answered.

Instead of pulling up to the gate and getting out, the limo pulled past the main gates and around to a smaller, more intimate runway, eventually stopping next to a private jet.

"Can you make it up the stairs?" D asked.

"I can try." Their moving a man hogtied and gagged into the plane would be scene enough without having D carry a weak woman in, too.

"That's my girl." D got out first. Giving her a hand out, he held her in place "Hang on a minute."

7 entered the aircraft and came back out again. He nodded to D. "Go on. It's safe."

The twelve steps made her Jello legs quake, and she hesitated.

"I can still carry you."

"I might need a push." She half teased but took the steps one at a time. At the top, a beautiful woman in a neat uniform greeted them. Natalia smiled then smelled the air. Fear racked her, and she stumbled back in her desperation to get away from the human.

D steadied her, keeping her from falling back down the stairs. "What is it?"

"She's human," she whispered, gripping the handrail.

D wrapped strong arms around her stomach, pulling her against his chest. "Like not all wolves are good, not all humans are bad. You can trust Z's staff. He trusts very few."

Passing them, carrying the tied-up wolf over his shoulders, Z said, "I don't even trust my brothers."

"True story," 7 added to the conversation.

As Natalia entered the cabin, the other woman stepped back, giving her the space she needed. "I'm sorry."

"Mr. Zames told us you have had a rough time. No apologies needed." She indicated the first two seats. "If you will get settled in, I believe the pilot has clearance to take off."

"Have you ever flown before?" D asked.

"Once, when we left America. I was very young. And it was nothing like this."

"Very few ever fly like this." D helped her with her seat belt. Instead of joining her, he headed to the back to talk with the others.

"Can I get you something to drink before we take off?" the flight attendant asked. "Perhaps something to take the edge off. A glass of wine?"

"Please." The other woman left only to return a few moments later with a glass of red liquid. "Thank you."

"My pleasure. Once we are in the air, I'll serve lunch. Sir, can I bring you anything?"

"Not just yet." D sat beside her as the plane began moving. "You doing okay?"

"I think so."

"Good. Z said there is a bedroom compartment in the rear. You can lie down, if you wish. It's a long flight. Z is going to talk to the pilot about finding a place for our layover where you can run."

"I don't want to be a problem."

"You aren't a problem. If Z is being hospitable, take it. Only his mate, Ripley, gets to see this side of him."

"Why is he being kind to me?"

"Because no one deserves the life you have led."

She took them up on the bed, but required D wrapped around her in order to relax. The layover in Iceland, where another black limo waited, proved a blessing. 7 and D escorted her to a deserted area where another infiltrator met them. 63, who had been in the country on assignment, took them to a safe area where they could run free for as long as they needed.

D stayed back, allowing her the distance she needed, although she could tell from his tension it went against everything in him to do so. She ran, sniffed, and stood up on a hill, allowing the wind to rush through her fur. Every time she felt lost, she turned to find him a few hundred feet behind, watching over her. She shifted back before she reached exhaustion, and D ushered her into the car and back to the plane.

"Perfect timing," Z said as they reentered the

plane.

D watched the clouds outside the window, but his mind roamed back to the field in Iceland. With the wind at her back, his mate experienced her first true steps of freedom. If they weren't rushing the clock, he would have bought her a place and allowed her to stay as long as she wanted. But they had to get back as soon as possible. Z placed a call to Drew, the Tao alpha, who said Natalie's grandfather had taken a turn for the worse. He had been hesitant to tell the older man of their discovery for fear of something holding them up in Lithuania.

Once they entered US airspace, they planned to break the news. Z informed Drew they had one of the many wolves Z hunted in custody, ready for a handoff at the border of Tao lands. Only one of them would be allowed to go in, and it needed to be D. Z was eager to head straight to Ripley's side.

"Will the others be joining us on Tao lands?" Natalie asked, fidgeting with the straw in her drink.

"Others?" Z didn't look up from his paperwork.

"Lenora, Balbus, the elephants, any of the other shifters?"

D reached over and grabbed her hand, her anxiety rolled off her in waves. "I am sure they are safe."

"But where did they go?" She couldn't believe it had taken her this long to think about the others. How selfish could she be? Now that she came down from her long run, the freedom she only now could appreciate opened her to a sense of guilt the others weren't with her.

"They won't be joining you on Tao lands." Z looked up. "They are all on an island off the coast of

Maine."

"Maine?"

"There's a spa on the island called the Wiccan Haus. Believe me they will be well taken care of."

"Can I call them? See them again?"

D looked at Z who shook his head. "You all need to heal. Perhaps after they are healthy we can arrange for you to see them again."

Natalie reached across the aisle and touched Z's arm. "Can you at least pass a message along to them that I am sorry I couldn't have done more for them?"

"Had it not been for you, they wouldn't have been rescued. You have nothing to feel sorry about." Z offered her a rare smile. "But I will pass along your message to the powers that be."

Her shoulders relaxed, and she leaned back into her chair seemingly content with his brother's answer. She accepted a set of headphones from the flight attendant. Once she settled in to watch a comedy and had let out a series of giggles, D turned back to the window and let his thoughts wonder to what the hell would happen next.

"What is the plan when we get there?" Natalie asked sometime later.

D turned away from the view out the window, he estimated they had about thirty minutes before they landed. "Once we land, we'll make our way to your grandfather's pack."

"I know that part. What about you?"

"I'll stay until I know you're settled then head out. My brothers and I aren't particularly welcome in town. Well, not trusted might be a better term."

"So you're leaving without me?"

"I am. You need your freedom, and I can't give

that to you when we're together."

"What if I don't want you to leave me?"

"You say so, now, and in the morning you'll complain and say I own you again." He brought her knuckles to his lips. "You need time, time with your kin, and time to be free."

"I can't sleep without you near."

"I am hoping it is the same as with the connection to my brother. As soon as I get far enough from you, your need to have me around will lessen."

He didn't hope for anything of the sort at all. He wanted to be with her, and the thought their connection could so easily be broken angered him. He handed her a card. Written on it was *D and S Consultants* and a phone number. "I'm only a phone call away."

"So I can call you whenever I need you?" She held the card tight, curling the edges.

"No, you may call me when you really need me, if you're in trouble, or have decided to truly be my mate." She needed space, and the only way for her to get it was to stop leaning on him. "I don't think I can be selfless again." Her grip on his arm tightened.

"Maybe I don't need my freedom."

"You're scared, and I think that fear is pretty normal. You're about to be thrown into a pack you don't remember, and they are going to act like you belong. You don't need to add a new mate to the mix. You've spent the majority of your life in a cage, under the thumb of evil people." He cupped her face and brought his lips to hers. "You deserve to live. Free."

They remained quiet as the plane landed because there wasn't anything more to be said.

Chapter Six

They opted for two large vehicles. 7 and Natalia in the first one. D drove the other one while Z focused on his prisoner. As they made their way down the road, curiosity finally got the better of her. "Why two cars?"

7 didn't take his eyes off the road. "The wolf has been on the run for a while now. He might have information on where others might be. A hint he might talk would be enough for some to hire someone to take him out before we get there."

"So why not have you drive Z and D with me?"

"Your guess is as good as mine," 7 answered. "I suspect since my idiot twin means to give you your freedom, he figured he should start as he meant to go on."

"I didn't ask him to leave. In fact, I asked him to stay."

"I'm aware of that. It's very difficult for either of us to hide anything from the other."

"Is he upset?"

"What do you think?" He took his eyes off the

road only long enough to throw her a look of pity. "He finally finds his mate, and she really isn't prepared to deal with having a mate. It's bound to hurt. But it isn't your fault."

"How can you say it's not my fault?"

"Because it's the truth."

"Yet, you are angry."

"I'm not angry as much as frustrated about the situation." 7 graced her with a slight smile.

"What do you two usually talk about when no one can hear you?"

"Usually, it's just regular conversations like we would have with anyone, just not aloud."

"What is he asking you now?"

"He wants to know if you are okay."

"What did you tell him?"

"I said, if he keeps asking me, I'll push you out of this moving vehicle so he can have something to be worried about."

"Nice." She giggled then paused. "You are joking, aren't you?"

"I did tell him that, but I promise I won't push you out...not while it's in motion, anyway."

"Thank you, I think." She gnawed her lower lip, working up the gumption to ask what she really needed to know. "Will he be okay?"

"Not at first, but, as time passes, it'll get easier to deal with. A few assignments to take his mind off you will help, and one day you'll wake up and need your mate. Fate rarely makes mistakes, and he'll be waiting for you."

"How can you be so sure?"

"Because that is how being mated works."

"Do you have a mate?"

"No, my people don't always find ours. We certainly don't hold out for them."

"But D and Z both found theirs?"

"Z married long ago and only discovered his mate this year. At the moment, I'm quite happy to be mateless. You and Ripley are enough to keep me crazy for years."

She watched the countryside in rapt anticipation, hills that appeared familiar yet foreign all at once. But, as 7 slowed the car for a turn, she saw a weather-beaten house on a hill. The two front windows were broken out, but it was the bare, covered porch that stretched the full front of the shabby old building that triggered memories long suppressed. "Stop."

"What?"

"Stop, please."

He pulled to the side of the road, and she jumped out. D slammed on the brakes, leapt out of the other car, and came to her side. "What are you doing?"

"I used to live here." She stepped forward, hesitant. "I remember this place."

"Go on up, Ryker's people are close by. We can do the handoff here as well as we could half a mile up the road," Z said, shutting the door and shifting.

Natalie sniffed the air. Familiar smells brought back memories in a rush. Playing on the porch, sleeping on a blanket on the floor before the fire.

"There is someone in the house," D said "Natalie, stop."

"Why?"

"The old lady who lived here died years ago."

In a second, everything went crazy. D shifted and ran full force for the house. She saw a flash of light in the dark recesses of the house aimed in her direction, and she braced herself for the impact that never came.

A woman's scream rent the air and the area smelled of gunpowder and blood. 7 crumpled to the ground at her feet, the snow around him turning red. "D! 7 is hurt."

He came out of the shack, dragging Shelley Testa behind him. He shifted back to human so quickly, she had to blink to believe it had happened. He grabbed the other woman's arms, ignoring the blood trickling over her fingers from damage hidden in her clothes. "7!"

D ripped the weapon from Shelley's hand and placed it in Natalia's palm. "If the bitch so much as coughs, shoot her." He kneeled beside his brother, assessing the damage. One second, 7 panted in human form, blood pooling around him, the next he shifted into wolf. D picked up the bullet from the ground and glared at the other woman. "You dare shoot at my mate and injure my brother?"

"He killed my husband."

Natalie pointed the gun at Shelley's head. "He deserved to die. You'll never hurt another person or shifter again."

"Give me the gun back," D said. "You aren't a killer. It isn't in you."

"She can't continue to hurt people, and that is all she will do, hurt people." Her hands shook, but her grip tightened on the gun. "How did you find us?"

"The old hag we bought you from here said you had family close by. Where else would you have gone? When I returned to the circus site and found it a ghost town, I knew Lee was dead. Didn't need a body to tell me. So I took the remaining money and hauled it out here. Got here an hour ago. I worried I'd missed you."

"Why? Why are you so hateful?"

"You are nothing but an animal, worthless in your abilities."

D tsked. "I might remind you she still has a gun on you."

"She won't use it."

"Maybe not, but I have no qualms of breaking your neck."

Shelley swallowed deeply as she moved a hand to her throat. "You can't just kill me."

"Give me one good reason, just one."

"Because if I die, my lawyer will release information to show the world of your kind. You can't risk publicity now, can you?"

D smiled, not the joyful smile he did around his brother or the playful one she had seen, this time he leered full of menace. "I think you should meet the boogeyman. Actually, I think you have met my brother Z."

Z stood behind them in wolf form, his black fur contrasted against the winter snow. He waited until he knew Shelley watched and shifted into the person she had thought would save them. "I'll take care of this one. I think Drew might want to deal with her as well."

"You are going to give Drew a swing?"

"Only if he wants to. Get 7 out of here, he needs medical attention. You need to take him back to our healers."

"But...." D didn't know where to go, she could tell.

"I can't take him. It has to be you, his twin," Z

said in a calm voice. For the first time, he sounded like a brother concerned and not some distant general barking orders. "I'll take Natalie to her grandfather. But 7 needs more than either the Tao or Greystones can offer."

Natalia hesitated; she didn't want him to leave but knew he had to. She wanted some freedom, but not like this. "D."

"Get to know your people. We have the rest of our lives. If you need me, I'll come to you."

"Can I come with you?"

7 huffed as D lifted him into his arms.

"No, not until we have permissions in place. Besides, your grandfather needs to see you."

"But...."

Z stepped between them. "There is no time, Natalie. 7 is bleeding. D needs to get him to our people. Only they can help him. And you need to finish your journey. Say your good-byes while I call for a helicopter."

D laid 7 in the back of the SUV. He dug into a bag and pulled out a shirt, ripping it into strips to tie around the wound. "Natalie, you know this is the only way. Z can get in touch with me if you need something."

"You won't come back, will you?"

"You'll never forgive yourself if you don't get to know your kin." He cupped her face and kissed her hard. "Until next time."

"I just sent you the meet-up coordinates," Z said, coming up to the car as D climbed into the driver's seat. "7, don't you dare die."

"Can't promise anything—" He broke off in a coughing fit.

Z slammed the door and D drove off, leaving Natalia to stare as he moved out of her life.

"We need to get going."

So much for the quick pity party she'd started. Z obviously wasn't having any of it. She wondered if he would be more sympathetic to his own mate. She allowed herself one last glance at the car, now far in the distance, before pulling her coat tight around her and following Z into the woods. "Why didn't you kill her the way you did Lee?"

"I don't kill indiscriminately. There are a lot of variables leading to what happened in Lithuania. Shelley is about to discover what a fate worse than death means. What happens to her now is in the hands of the Tao pack."

A large man greeted them at what she believed must be the edge of the Tao lands. He didn't say much of anything but took Shelley into his custody before turning to Natalie. "Welcome home." He nodded at Z. "Infiltrator."

"Enforcer," Z said in turn.

Tension could be cut with a knife until finally a woman stepped forward. So overwhelmed by the other man, Natalia hadn't noticed another person around.

"Hi, Natalie. I'm Jenna, here to escort you to your grandfather. He's very excited to meet you." Jenna gave her a big smile but cut her eyes to the infiltrator.

"Are you coming?" Wary to leave the only person she knew, she prayed Z would say yes.

"I'll take you as far as town. I need to meet with Drew, but my mate is pregnant, and it has been weeks since I've been with her. I'm anxious to get home."

"You'll be safe here. The pack isn't what it was when you were a child." Jenna placed a reassuring hand on her arm.

"I honestly don't remember much of anything from my childhood here." She remembered the house, and when she mentioned it, 7 got shot. Perhaps remembering wasn't a good thing. The large man took Shelley in the opposite direction. "Where are they going?"

"Ryker is our pack enforcer, and he is taking her away from town. It's better that way." She flashed Natalia a reassuring smile. "We have a bit of a walk. I suggest we shift to cover the distance more quickly."

She bit her lip, once again reminded of her difference.

"Be honest with the pack about everything. Do not try to impress anyone. Nothing that happened to you was your fault," Z stated. "D isn't here. In his place, I'll be at your flank."

She nodded then addressed Jenna. "I'm still getting my wolf legs. My life has been on a tight leash. They never allowed us to run."

"Then we use two legs." Jenna led the way down a trail for another hundred feet before taking a path Natalia never would have noticed otherwise.

Both of these wolves could make the trek in less than half the time it would take them to do so in human form. But she couldn't handle it if Z was forced to carry her the rest of the way. She wanted to stride into town on her own legs. For the first time in her memory, she didn't have someone in control of her life. "I can leave whenever I want?"

"You can. I can't imagine Drew would hold you if

95

you didn't want to be here. Although he might try to persuade you to stay at least until your grandfather dies," Z remarked.

"Wow. Do all infiltrators take courses in sensitivity, or is it just you?" The other woman stopped in her tracks, turning on Z.

Z stopped and stared Jenna down until she took a step back. "Would it be better to lie to her? The whole reason Drew asked me to find her was to grant a dying man's last wish."

"There are softer ways to say things."

"I've never known softness," Natalia whispered. D had said his kind weren't welcome in town. She would ask Z about it later. For now, she wasn't about to allow anyone to malign the man who'd saved her from hell. "I'm not sure what you have against infiltrators, but if it weren't for this man, I'd still be in a cage, and I can guarantee there would be two elephants and a bear who would be dead right now."

Jenna frowned as if unable to reconcile the man Natalia described with the traits she believed inherent in infiltrators. "We were told your life was hard but given no information to the conditions."

"I haven't seen your alpha to fill him in yet. Whatever Natalie chooses to tell anyone is up to her." Z indicated they needed to move on. "Natalie, don't speak too kindly of me. I quite prefer the fear I instill over admiration."

"You would."

"Ah, the twins must have been telling stories again."

She stopped and turned. "7 is going to be all right, isn't he? I never wanted anyone hurt because of me."

He glanced back the way they'd come. "I can't lie; he's in trouble. When he shifted, it should have healed the outside, but he is more than likely bleeding internally. The copter is taking them to an airfield where one of our healers will meet them and take them to the pack lands. He is in very good hands. If I thought for a second he couldn't make the trip, I would have demanded Ryker take him into town for one of their healers to take care of him."

"Why didn't you do that anyway?" Jenna demanded.

It did seem strange to send his brother hours in another direction when healers could be found within a half an hour. "Infiltrators have...unique needs."

"That's all you are going to tell me, isn't it?"

"Yep."

"Damn, you are frustrating." She didn't miss the slight upturn of Z's lips.

They continued the rest of the way in silence. As they came through the tree line, a small town came into view, the main street a strange mix of disrepair and renovation. As they approached, everyone moved out of Z's way. They whispered and shot him looks of distrust, all except one, a young man who exuded confidence and command.

"Natalie, or do you prefer Natalia?"

No one had actually asked her preference before. "I have always gone by Natalia, but perhaps a change is in order. Maybe Nat?"

"Nat, it is. I'm Drew, the Tao alpha." He extended a hand. "You have been missed."

"I wish I could say I remember this, any of this."

"I remember you, as does my mate, Betty. She says as a toddler you always ran. Ran everywhere."

97

Running. Something she couldn't do now without falling over.

"You will run again. You simply need time." He turned his attention to Z. "I'm going to take her to her grandfather. We can catch up at Gee's when I'm done."

Z gave Natalie a wink. "It's been a pleasure, and I'm sure I'll see you again."

He didn't mention anything about his brother being her mate. She realized he gave her the choice, he, as D, allowed her her freedom. "Thank you."

"Your grandfather lives on the edge of town," Drew explained as they passed the remains of a burned building, the faint scent of soot lingering even after what she was sure was at least months. "He is...."

"Dying. I know." Mixed emotions ran through her: fear, nervousness, excitement, and anxiety. "I'll do my best to make this easy on him."

"We've told him what little we know. I'm not telling you to lie, but what would the whole truth do to him?" He paused outside the door. "Do you want me to go in with you?"

She shook her head. She didn't need a stranger introducing her to another stranger. The only one she wanted by her side was D, and that thought caught her off guard.

"I'll leave you, then. Gee has a room prepared for you above his bar. At the moment, we don't have any empty cabins."

"It'll be fine." He didn't need to hear she'd lived in a cage for the last decade. She knocked on the door and waited until she heard a soft, gravelly voice bidding her enter then centered herself and opened the door.

Sitting in a chair in the darkened room, an elderly man stared at her expectantly. A threadbare blanket lay over his legs. His hand shook as he reached for her. "My Natalie, you are so much like your mother, I would know you anywhere."

His voice brought a flood of memories back. "Gamps."

She moved into his arms with love, and they cried together.

Chapter Seven

Days turned into weeks with no word from D. Z had left immediately following his meeting with Drew, unwilling to be away from his mate for another day. She had hoped being away from D would have allowed her feelings for him to wane, but her need and desire had grown stronger. And absence really did seem to make the heart grow fonder.

Her grandfather passed away a couple of days after she arrived. He had answered some questions about her young life but, more important, had died content in the knowledge she had made it home safely. She hadn't told him the gory details of her incarceration. It would have done neither of them any good. She had only wished for time with the man. She remained above the bar. Though her grandfather had left her the shack, the old building looked about ready to fall in upon itself. In the end, she told Drew he could do with it as he saw fit.

In one of their meetings, Drew explained why D hadn't returned, despite an open invitation to visit. Due to 7's medical injuries and D being the only one with his blood type, he could not leave his side. She understood. But understanding didn't make it any easier. Eventually Z arrived to meet with the alpha, but all he would say was, "7's still healing, and D sends his best."

She tried to help out where she could but, so far, hadn't found a job to fit her nonexistent skills. No need for a circus animal in the pack. So she cleaned what she could for Gee, although he insisted her room and board had been more than paid for. By whom, she could only guess because the bear had proven to be as tight-lipped at times as Z. The local teacher worked with her to improve her reading and writing, and the town's women had come together to make sure she had the essentials. But she still felt like an outsider.

"Nat, you have a package," Gee said as she descended the old wooden staircase.

A plain brown box rested at the end of the bar. "Me?"

"Jenna brought it in this morning. She found it in the old hag's abandoned shack as she was doing her morning rounds."

The top of the box simply stated, *Natalie.*

Gee came over with a knife and slit the seal. Although it took her some time, she managed to read the note inside without too much trouble.

Dear Natalie,

I am so sorry I couldn't come for your grandfather's funeral. I tried to make it back, but situations beyond my control prevented me getting to you. I am enclosing items to make life easier for you. I want you to have whatever freedom you choose. If you need anything from me, use the cell phone enclosed and press the D. I will come. I think of you daily but have vowed to give you the space you have never had.

7 is well on his way to being his old self. But it will take time.

Could you please give the small box in the bottom to Gee, (unopened)?

Run free.

Yours,

D

She dug into the package and pulled out a surprisingly heavy smaller box with Gee's name and a quick *thank you* scrawled on top. "Gee, I'm to give this to you unopened."

The bear licked his lips, took the box, and disappeared into the kitchen. She removed the cell phone and placed it to the side, for fear she would call him right away. The clothes she'd chosen but left behind at the safe house in Lithuania lay neatly folded within plastic zipper bags. Underneath the clothes, she found a black wallet with the letter N embroidered in red. She opened it and gasped. Inside lay more money than she had ever seen in her life. Another note lay with the bills. *Run where the need takes you.* Three credit cards and a photo ID filled the slotted pockets.

With freedom in the palm of her hand, she suddenly knew it didn't mean a thing if she couldn't share her new adventures with him.

"Gee?"

The bear stuck his head out of the kitchen.

"How would I find D?"

"Z would know."

"How would I find Z?"

"Ripley would know."

She groaned. "And how would I find Ripley?"

"Now, that one I know. She is at the Greystone River company compound. Do you want me to see about getting you a ride out there?"

The next day, she found herself getting out of an old battered truck in the empty parking lot of the business whose sign stated they were closed for the season with a phone number and web address for further information. A soft light glowed from within the small office. She grabbed her bag and waved good-bye to the driver. The door opened, and a heavily pregnant woman came out. "Can I help you?"

"Yes, I'm trying to find Ripley."

"You've found her." The other woman sniffed the air as her face lit up with a smile. "You're D's mate."

It wasn't a question but a statement. "Can you still smell him on me?"

"I can."

The idea thrilled her and helped understand why not one man at Los Lobos even flirted with her. When she had first arrive one of the women who came into the bar had made a comment that all the unmated wolves would be all over her. Yet not once had one looked at her twice. "I hoped you can tell me where I might find him."

"Did you call him?"

"I wanted to see him. Talk to him face-to-face." She shivered a bit as the sun hid behind the clouds.

"Come on in." Ripley urged her into the building, closing the door behind them. "Excuse the mess. I am, as my sisters like to say, 'nesting,' which means I keep taking everything down trying to reorganize this damned space. Can I offer you something to drink?"

"No thank you."

"All right, then. I suppose getting to know each other will have to wait until you and D reunite." She reached for a yellow walkie-talkie. "Z, honey."

"Yeah, baby," Z responded immediately.

"Can you tell me where your brothers are?"

"At the moment, they should be doing 7's physical therapy out in the open field. But that remains to be seen."

"Thanks." She returned the device to its charging unit and turned. "Shall we?"

"He's here?" Somehow, she'd imagined he was off in some super-secret spy-like hidden lair built inside a mountain where only infiltrators could find it. Never had it occurred to her he would be a few hours away from Los Lobos, hanging out at a rafting company.

Ripley grinned wide. "Well, not here, exactly. He is about fifteen minutes from here near the family compound." The pregnant wolf grabbed her keys off a hook by the door, threw a coat on, and waited at the door. "You coming?"

"I'm nervous."

"I don't know everything going on. Z, as you might have figured out, isn't very forthcoming with information. Neither are the twins. But I know D has been, against his better judgment, giving you your freedom. He arrived here a couple of weeks ago, and I see him staring off in the direction of Los Lobos, his fists clenched tight as he fights the need to be with you."

"I asked for my freedom." She also asked him to

stay, but perhaps her need for space was what he heard loudest.

"Of course you did. You've never had it." She picked up Natalie's bag and exited. "Close the door behind you."

She liked Ripley already. She followed the other woman into the Jeep. "So he's been here for a while?"

"Since they gave 7 the okay to travel." She climbed into the truck with a humph and mumbled something about her belly. She reached over and touched the wallet Nat held within tight hands. "I see you got his package."

"How did you know?"

Ripley reversed the Jeep and drove down the bumpy road but didn't seem to care they were jostled all over the place. "You don't think a man would have thought that up on his own? He wanted to help but didn't know how, and Lord knows Z wasn't helpful. I suggested he send you something."

"Oh." Here she thought he was so romantic.

"Everything in the box was his idea. I just gave the push. I think he needed assurance it was okay to reach out." She patted Nat's knee. "It gave him something to do, to work on."

"What's it like to be mated to an infiltrator?"

She shrugged. "I have nothing to compare it to really. But I figure I've more freedom than most. He travels a lot. You have to accept you'll never know his deepest secrets. He can't tell you where he is. You have to trust more than I think most do."

She tapped a button on the visor and a bush slid to the side. "Used to be an open dirt road. Z didn't approve. There are no fences. This is just to keep out lost tourists or hunters. I didn't want you thinking you were closed in."

"Thank you."

"I'll have a room made up for you for the night. It's yours as long as you want it."

"Where does D stay?"

"As of tonight, I assume with you." She gave her a sassy grin. "He's to the north through the trees. Go to him as your wolf. It'll give you power. Trust her to lead you."

She swallowed the lump in her throat. This woman, who wore her strength like a banner, gave her hope of what she could become. Gee had suggested the Greystone betas might show her strength, but she had no idea what he'd meant. "I'll try."

"That's all any of us can do." Ripley got out of the Jeep and grabbed Nat's bag again.

"Should you be carrying something heavy?" She indicating the other woman's extended belly. She didn't know a lot about pregnant women, but she did know they weren't supposed to carry much.

"Pftt."

The compound consisted of five large buildings surrounding the perimeter, with smaller cottages sprinkled throughout and a larger building in the center. Children played in the snow, and, although the adults stood nearby, a sense of safety and harmony infused the entire place. Two women waved at her, another approached to argue with Ripley in vain, trying to get a hold of the bag she carried.

Then the wind blew. Natalie caught a hint of his scent on the breeze, shifted, and ran like the devil followed on her heels. Through the woods, without hitting a single branch, she made it to the outskirts of the open field. He stood thirty yards away in a blue T-shirt and jeans, while 7 lunged for him in wolf form. They both halted mid-attack and turned. D shifted in a second and became a black blur heading her way. He stopped a breath away and rubbed his head against hers before shifting back. She fell into his arms as soon as the last bit of her wolf disappeared.

"I've missed you," he breathed into her hair.

Warmth and a sense of belonging washed over her as his heart beat like a cadence in her ear against his chest. "Have you been waiting here for me long?"

"All my life." He cupped her cheeks, forcing her to look at him before he kissed her hard. The cold no longer affected her as his warmth filled her. She wrapped her arms around his waist, pulling him closer. When he eased back, he stared at her a moment before speaking. "Tell me my wait is over."

She nodded and lifted up on tiptoe to touch her lips to his again. "We have waited long enough. I discovered freedom is empty without you to share it with."

"You are determined to give me diabetes." 7 gripped her upper arm. "Good to see you, Natalie."

"You, too, 7." He looked good, not like someone who took a bullet a few weeks back. "How are you feeling?"

"Like someone put a piece of lead into my shoulder. Not 100 percent, yet, but if D has anything to do with it, I will be in record time."

D cleared his throat.

"I think that's D's way of saying get lost. Interesting, as you could have screamed into my brain and she never would have known." 7 grabbed his coat. "See you later...or maybe not."

Silence reigned between them. Despite all the time she had spent playing this moment in her head, the words she had planned to say blew from her memory. It had to do with how she missed him. He stared over her shoulder in the direction his brother had gone, and he waited. After a minute, he twitched and took a deep breath.

"7 out of reach now?"

"He is."

"It's hard on you, isn't it?" She cupped his cheek. "When you can't sense him anymore."

He nodded, moving into her palm. "It's like someone cuts off a part of you. Until the night we helped you escape, I didn't know we could break the connection with distance."

"You had never been apart?"

"Never. It was what made our abilities useful. We have amazing agility and speed, but so do all infiltrators. Even if we are a bit faster, it didn't make us any more useful than anyone else, but we are two wolves who could act as one."

"Allowing for double coverage no one else could detect."

"Allowing for double trouble. We have caused more mayhem than any two wolves could." He kissed her palm before leaning in to kiss her lips. "But, when you are never alone, it's strange to have silence."

"I know it's not the same, but I think I understand. I was never alone, not really, and it was never quiet. I thought I needed to be by myself, and, in freedom, discover peace."

"But you didn't?"

"No, it only brought me emptiness. What I longed for was a sense of belonging. A family."

Pain washed over his face, "Oh, I didn't ask about how you are holding up since your grandfather died."

"I would've loved to have known him, but he's still essentially a stranger to me. I enjoyed the time I had with him. Would have loved more but he died happy."

He groaned, throwing his head back in frustration. "I should've been there for you."

"It's hard to be somewhere when you are in a hospital bed, acting as a human blood bank. It's I who should've been there for you. 7 was in worse shape than you let on when you left Los Lobos."

"I didn't want you to worry more than you already were. I didn't lie. I just didn't tell you the whole truth. It was touch-and-go for a week. But you needed to be there for your grandfather and for you. If you hadn't known someone loved you...."

"I wouldn't have realized I loved you?"

"Say that again."

"I realized I loved you. At first, I thought it was this mating thing.'"

"Mating thing?"

His irritation at her description brought a smile to her face. "Connection...better?"

"Much."

"As I was saying, at first, I thought I just missed you because of our connection. But as I suddenly had everything I thought I wanted, the one thing I realized I needed was you."

"I have never felt"—he pounded his chest in emphasis—"so split on where and when I needed to be somewhere. Driving away might be the hardest thing I ever did. But I knew Los Lobos couldn't help

7, and I knew you couldn't come to my pack with me."

"I have to be given permission."

He nodded.

"Gee told me. So...."

"So?"

"When are you going to find us someplace warm and private and make love to me the way a mate deserves?"

"I thought you would never ask." He grabbed her hand and pulled her behind him. When she tripped trying to keep up, he paused only long enough to lift her into his arms and carry her. "Hell, I have no idea where to go."

"The empty cabin on the east side of the compound. Ripley says it's Natalie's as long as she wants it." Z, leaning against a tree, nearly caused Natalie to jump out of her skin, but it seemed his presence had no effect on her mate. He nodded in acknowledgment and picked up his pace.

She clung to him, laying her head on his shoulder and closing her eyes. He slowed, and she sensed the buildings around her. She also could feel eyes on her as he carried this strange woman through the center of the compound to their lodgings.

"Open your eyes," he whispered into her hair after closing the door behind him.

She did and gasped. The large log cabin room took her breath away. The amber beams reached high into the air as if Ripley knew small, confined spaces made her nervous. He lowered her to her feet, and she tried to ignore the large four-poster bed in the corner made of the same wood as the house. The room glowed under the light of the dozens of candles burning and the blaze of the fire in the hearth. A basket of food lay open on the table near the fireplace. Her bag was placed on the hardwood floor next to the dresser. "I didn't expect this."

"The Greystones know how to make their guests feel welcome. It's why they are so good at what they do."

"Do all the cabins look like this?"

"No, Ripley and Z's is very simple and small with lots of skylights. She loves to see the stars. And 7 and I stay in a dorm-like building on the opposite side of the camp."

"Will you be staying there now?" she asked, biting her thumbnail.

"This is your home now, so you tell me. Am I staying across the courtyard in a cold, lonely bed, or am I staying here where I belong, next to my mate."

She sidled up next to him. "Put like that, it's an easy decision to make."

"I hope so because my feelings for you are anything but easy, and there is only one place I need to be." He lowered his head to capture her lips. Her heart thumped so hard and so loud she suspected he could hear it, too. She lifted a hand to his chest to discover his heart beat as hard as hers.

His hands worked the hem of her shirt up so he could grip her bare waist. The skin-to-skin touch sizzled, and she sucked in her breath.

"You okay?" he asked.

"I forgot what your touch does to me."

"We can wait, take this slow."

"No, I need this, need you."

"If, at any time, it's too much, you tell me, and we'll stop."

She pulled back to really look at him. "But that's not fair to you."

"This isn't about me; this is about you." His thumb brushed over her lower lip. "I didn't understand what it's like to care more about someone else than myself until I held you in my arms."

"What about 7?"

"It's different. 7 and I have always been one and the same. We are the 'twins.' But I split from him to protect you. Had it been anyone but my mate, I wouldn't have broken the twin connection."

"I don't ever want him to feel like he isn't welcome."

"He wouldn't have taken a bullet for you if 7 held any misgivings about us."

"I don't want to think about violence or shootings tonight. Right now, I just need to be with my mate." She pulled his T-shirt up and over his head, marveling at the hard muscles beneath. His stomach could have been chiseled from stone.

His warm skin sent tingling through her fingertips. She allowed her wolf to take over, leading her and giving her strength she wouldn't normally have. She left a trail of kisses from his shoulder up his neck to his jawline. His breath caught as she kissed the soft spot under his ear. She pulled away glancing down at his balled fists at his sides. "Why aren't you touching me?"

"I am trying to allow you time to explore, to feel comfortable with me before I lose control. She reached down and brought his hand to her breast. "Touch me. I don't want this to be only about me. I want this to be about us. Our needs."

"Do you understand what will happen, I have to

rein in my beast tonight, for your sake. I want to make this special and give you as much pleasure as possible, but if I'm not gentle, I could hurt you."

"I'm told it will hurt anyway."

"There are ways of minimizing the sting."

"Oh, and how would you know these things? Have you slept with a great many virgins?" She wasn't stupid enough to think there hadn't been other women, but she didn't wanted to think about it.

"No, but this pack is full of them, women, not virgins, well, they all used to be virgins. I'm making a mess of this. Let's just leave it."

"You asked them how to deflower a virgin?" Shock mixed with a good dose of embarrassment washed over her.

"Who better to ask than a woman?"

Something in his statement made all her doubts and concerns disappear. He cared enough to learn, through what couldn't have been easy conversations, how best to help her discover sex. He stood there rigid, delaying any gratification on his part so she could experience what she needed. "What did they say?"

"They informed me, under the patient hand of a skilled lover, the breaking of your hymen could be done in a way to lessen the pain and still bring pleasure." As he spoke, his hand moved lower and cupped her mound. "If I treat your virginity as a gift more precious than gold, then you'll understand how blessed I feel at being the one to take it from you."

"You can't take what is freely given."

His lips covered hers, and she moaned, rubbing herself against his hand, needing the pressure of his fingers through the fabric. So frantic, she didn't notice he had unbuttoned her jeans until the warmth of his palm against her belly brought her heat soaring. And before she could think, he deepened the kiss and rubbed her clit. He could lead her anywhere, and she would have followed, so when he urged her backward until the wall was at her back, she didn't complain. When he withdrew, she whined, but only until she realized he eased her pants down her hips over her thighs and off. Warm lips worked back up her legs, forcing them apart. He ripped the barrier of her underwear from her then grasped the half-moons of her ass, bringing her to him for a feast. His tongue circled her clit until she shuddered, and only then did his tongue enter her.

On tiptoe, she fought for control and the ecstasy she yearned for. "Only when you figure out what I am spelling can you come."

"What?" Brought out of her light-headed desire to orgasm, she stared down at him.

He nipped her inner thigh. "Figure out what I am spelling with my tongue, and I will give you everything you have ever wanted."

His mouth returned to her and she moaned. "I don't know."

He repeated the motion. With a gasp, she managed a B. Then, "E. M. I. I don't know...M." He stopped and shook his head before returning to try again. "N. E. Fuck me, yes. 'Be mine.'"

The room spun as he lifted her into his arms and carried her to the bed. As he placed her on the mattress, she removed her shirt and bra. He followed, stripping off his pants. The next thing she knew, he lay between her legs, holding his weight up with his arms. "Are you sure?"

"I have never been more sure about any single thing in my life. You're my other half."

"Thank the goddess." He rubbed the tip of his cock against the wet opening to her womb. She lifted her hips in frustration. With one hand, he forced her back down, holding her hip in place against the bed. "I know you want this, but if you aren't careful, you will hurt yourself. We have to take this slow."

She looked up at him and nodded. She wanted it done. She didn't like to be weak and worried her virginity made her fragile. In the camp, her virginity had been a commodity Lee had threatened to sell to the highest bidder. D, on the other hand, even at the expense of his personal comfort, gave her all the time she needed.

"I want you to take a deep breath and let it out." He kissed her neck, giving her something new to focus on. "Breathe."

She did and, on the third exhale, he entered her with one stroke causing her to clench, catch her breath, and wish she hadn't been so anxious to get rid of her virginity. She could taste the blood where her teeth broke through the skin of his shoulder as she bit down in pain. "Keep breathing."

He moved a little, and she clenched around him, stopping him with her legs. "Not yet."

He panted and nodded. Sweat beaded on his brow, and she realized he fought the need to continue. "What do I do?"

He snapped his head up. "Relax."

She filled her lungs until they hurt and focused on relaxing as she exhaled. By the fourth try, she finally allowed her knees to fall open. "I'm ready."

"You sure?"

She nodded and lifted up to kiss him. When he kissed her, she didn't think about anything but him, but when he moved within her this time, the discomfort disappeared, leaving a sensation of fullness. And then the fullness brought with it pleasure. A sense of being together. Her wolf howled and she called his name, urging him on, wanting all of him, needing to feel him deep inside her where his seed would cement their bond.

As he reached between them and rubbed her clit, he lit fireworks within her. From the pit of her stomach, the sparks lit, and shudders racked her all the way to her toes. She threw back her head. Her world erupted around her. He brushed away the hair from her face and gently grazed her forehead with his lips.

"Hang on." Only when she nodded and gripped his shoulders did he pick up a pace she couldn't imagine. The headboard hit the wall behind them with such force she feared it would split the wood in two. But then his wolf called to her, and she knew what he needed. She knew every thrust, how to counter in the exact angle to bring him the most pleasure, and when to hold him tight and ride the wave. In the end, when pleasure racked his body, she held tight, enjoying the glow of knowing she brought him to the heights of ecstasy.

When he collapsed on top of her, she clung, running her nails up his spine, listening to his breathing as he came down from his orgasm. She fought him when he went to move off her, but, even in his weakened state, she was no match for him.

"Are you okay?" he asked, pulling her into his side.

"I think so."

They lay there for a few minutes before he got up, went to the attached bathroom only to return with a washcloth, taking great care to clean himself off her. "I have a bath running, let's go get in."

"If you ran a bath, why the washcloth?"

"Because you are my responsibility." He lifted her from the bed and carried her in to the other room. He kissed her gently as he lowered her into the soothing warmth of the water. "I'll be right back. Do not fall asleep."

"Don't leave." Fear of the unknown enveloped her.

"I'm only going to get you something to drink. I can't leave you, don't you understand?" He squatted next to the tub. "It killed me to walk away from you in the Black Hills. Do you think I can do it again? Let me make sure you understand I can't."

"I can't help this feeling you are going to leave me."

"We are mates. You accepted your wolf side, and she accepted me."

"Why am I so nervous?"

"Because, right now, you are overwhelmed. When Ripley and Z first mated, she had to touch him all the time. She needed the connection to ground her. It took weeks before he could leave for more than a couple of hours."

"Now he leaves her for weeks at a time." Panic filled her. She didn't know if she could go days again, let alone weeks.

"And he always returns."

"But he leaves."

He reached for her, and, in an instant, she

calmed. "I can't promise I won't leave on some assignment for Z sometime, but it won't be anytime soon, and it won't be for more than a couple of days."

"What about your pack?"

"I've accepted a temporary banishment. We mutually decided." He stood. "You are my pack."

"Banishment?"

"It was that or I had to stay and finish my time in the filing room. Had I stayed, it would have been years before either 7 or I saw the light of day." As he leaned over to turn off the water, he offered her a smile. "We're both happy to be here and not there."

"Be patient with me."

"You have my entire life. Be right back." He left, whistling. She knew he did it to reassure her he was nearby. He returned, a bottle of wine in hand, and climbed into the oversized tub behind her. "Sorry I couldn't find glasses." He took a swig then handed it to her."

"Romantic."

"I am nothing if not classy."

Long past the time their skin pruned and the water cooled, they left the intimacy of their tub and moved back into bed now made up with clean sheets. "I feel silly lying in bed in the middle of the day when everyone is out and about."

"Please do this for me. If we leave this room before tomorrow morning, I will get razzed about my manliness for years."

"Oh, so my lying in bed all day with you will save your reputation?"

"Most definitely."

"It's a small request for my mate." She kissed his nipple and reveled in the shiver it induced. "Can I ask for something in return?"

"Anything."

"I want to run tonight."

He rolled onto his side so they lay face-to-face. "Your wolf?"

"She is stronger now. I'm learning to trust her, and she has to be allowed out."

"As soon as the sun goes down, I'll take you to a place where you're safe and you can run and test out your limits. I'll be there to pick you up or press you on."

"I know you will."

He leaned in and kissed her. "But, until then, we have a couple of hours to kill."

"What do you have in mind?"

"If you aren't too sore...."

"We wolves heal quickly."

"Thank the goddess for that." His mouth descended on hers, and the world receded as the two of them became one.

One heart, one soul, one mating.

About the Author

Award-winning author Dominique Eastwick grew up a US Navy Brat, so if there was a naval base, that was probably home. She currently resides in North Carolina with her husband, two children, crazy lab and lazy cat.

Dominique's love of reading started when she was told to read *To Kill a Mockingbird* in high school. A book that opened her eyes to the joys of reading and entering into the world of the author. To this day she ranks this book as her favorite.

Stay connected with my Newsletter:

http://eepurl.com/brjq6D

Also by Dominique

Strawberry Kisses
The Duke and the Virgin
The Marquis and the Mistress
The Earl and His Virgin Countess
Infiltrating Her Pack
Shifting Hearts
Siren's Serenade
Healing His Soul's Mate
Breaking the Mating Bond

www.ingramcontent.com/pod-product-compliance
Lightning Source LLC
Chambersburg PA
CBHW060938120626
46557CB00003B/1056